The Girl Who Hid in the Trees

Steve Stred

The Girl Who Hid in the Trees
Steve Stred
2019, 1st Edition
Cover art by Mason McDonald
Copy Edited by David Sodergren
Foreword by Gavin Kendall
Goodreads link:

https://www.goodreads.com/book/show/43255766-the-girl-who-hid-in-the-trees

Special thanks to these kind folks for their continued support and for taking the time to read this before the official release date!

Jodi Stredulinsky, Mason McDonald, Gavin Kendall, Trish Duppereault, Jessica Foster, Joe Zito, Sonora Taylor, Peter Lush, Michael Patrick Hicks, Toni Miller, Jim Coniglio, Mitch Meredith, Toni Le Compte, David Sodergren, Alex Pearson, Carissa Lovold, Sam Brunke-Kervin, Matias Rojo Ruilova, Rachel Drenning, Clota Wilkerson, Michelle Rubio, Diamond Kennedy, Cassie Daley, Shane Norton, Tracy Robinson, Bo Chappell, Suzy Michael, Becca Futrelli, Valerie Dorsey, Calvin Demmer, Deborah K. Hundt, Brandy Marie, Debra Gillis, Lauren Dunn, Miranda Crites, Warren Furnival, Justin M. Woodward, Zachary Walters, Cody Tidwell, Jake Foster, and Luke @luke.what.im.reading,

Foreword

I can pinpoint the first-time I discovered horror to approximately 1982. I would have been 10 and my father had a bookshelf overflowing with paperbacks. It was this collection of books that opened a door and triggered a love for reading. It was here I discovered Zane Grey Westerns, Edgar Rice Burroughs' Tarzan, and Richard E Howard's Conan. They all had gorgeous covers and looked like they'd been read hundreds of times. I never read any of these bar the synopsis. What I read were the darker looking books on the bottom row of the bookshelf. The small collection of some 15 or so books with black spines, the brief flash of colour on these books, yellows, reds ...perfect for eyes, teeth, claws and BLOOD. These books were my introduction to murder, ghosts, monsters & death. This was my introduction to horror. This was the jackpot for an impressionable ten year old mostly all made up of yellowing Pan Books of Horror and were the catalyst for my love of the genre.

The first horror novel I read is probably the same for most horror fans my age. The Rats. My now 12 year old self devoured the James Herbert classic with its easy to read prose, gut wrenching scenes of violence and gore, the excitement of sex scenes that would have certainly meant the book would have been banned by my mother yet she was OK with a man being torn limb from limb by rodents. Funny old world. I wasn't a voracious reader back then but the lurid, sleazy violence of Richard Laymon and Shaun Hutson kept me turning pages over the next few years.

I was 15 when my life changed forever. I'd read a book unlike anything I'd read before. Powerful, eloquent, visceral, life changing. Clive Barkers: Books of Blood set me on the path I'm on today. He is the one true constant in my reading life. The Books of Blood are the best collection of stories ever compiled. I just can't see anyone bettering it. It's that search for a better collection that has led me to this point.

I find myself in a very fortunate position where I'm able to channel my passion for Horror via my blog. Here I review books, interview authors and publishers and much more. This blog is where I have one true aim; to Promote Horror, to be part of, and develop a community where bloggers/reviewers work together to help authors and publishers. To help the people that may have the very effect on my children as those authors that featured on my father's bookshelves had on me.

I've interacted with many authors since the blog opened its doors in January 2017. It's a genuine thrill to talk to people that have written books I've read, to ask them questions about plots and the writing process. It was one such conversation that I had the pleasure of talking to Steve Stred.

Steve is a talent. He writes stories that wreak havoc with all your emotions. Stunning imagery, gore and violence abound but always with a purpose, never salacious. Wonderful characterisation and a wicked sense of humour. One of his stories featured a woman who took her false teeth out to prepare for a sexual encounter. I asked him why he made her do this as I found it all so delightfully warped. He answered 'because it's worse'. I felt this was the perfect answer. As a writer he's as adept at breaking the reader's heart as he is one of his characters heads. He writes stories you'll want to read because he can.

And it's one of these stories you are now holding in your hands. The Girl Who Hid in the Trees is a sumptuous tale that offers a lot of what Steve does so well. It's a tale to read late at night, to savour. With this story Steve's created a new Urban Legend that deserves to be talked about around campfires with a torch alight under your chin.

I have absolutely no doubt in my mind that Steve Stred is going to be one of those authors that a young reader will discover (possibly via a parents bookshelf) and in reading him a spark will ignite, setting them off on the journey of being a lifelong fan of Horror.

I just hope they get in touch if they ever find a collection better than the Books of Blood.

- Gavin Kendall, UK, January 2019

Prologue

August 5, 1884

"Abigail, don't stray too far, ok?"

Abigail heard her mom but ignored her. After all, she was now seven years old, and could take care of herself.

She walked through the deep grass beside McConnell's Forest, plucking petals from the daisy she had picked.

"He loves me, he loves me not. He loves me, he loves me not," she sung as she casually strolled away from their camp site.

It wasn't until she had plucked all the petals off the flower and discarded it over her shoulder that she realized she had wandered down the path into the woods. She turned around and around, scared, finding she was lost and unable see her mom.

"Mom?" She called out feebly.

"Mom? Please mom?"

She heard a noise close by.

"Hello?"

Abigail took a few steps towards the sound, and spotted yellowed eyes watching her from behind a bush.

"Who's there?"

She watched with awe as a girl close to her age danced out from behind the foliage and smiled at her. Her teeth matched the color of her eyes, yellow and dark. Her dress was caked in filth and mud. But the girl smiled and waved.

"Hello, who are you? Can you help me find my mom?" Abigail asked.

The girl giggled and turned, walking down the path away from Abigail, the morning sun cascading a bright aura around her.

"Please, please help me," she cried out, rushing towards the girl.

Then she was gone. Disappeared.

"What? No, where did you go? Please help me?" She called out.

From behind her the voice sang out.

"*Help you? But no one helped me. Now we count, one, two,*
three."

Abigail didn't feel any pain as the girl ripped her spine from her
body.

The girl left Abigail there in the path and disappeared into the
trees as though she'd never even been there.

1.

I first heard the urban legend when I was eight. My older brother Mikey and his friends were talking about it, and because I always tried to hang out with the group of teenagers, I heard them talking.

"No way, it's just a fucking story," Mikey angrily said. "There's no proof. No proof."

I hadn't seen my brother this angry since he caught me trying to steal one of his smokes. He punched my shoulder so hard my dad ended up taking me to get it x-rayed.

"Dude, it's true. Just cuz you're a bitch and too scared to go see for yourself, doesn't mean it's not true." Frankie always tried to get my brother going, trying to work him up. I couldn't stand Frankie, but that was because he smelled gross. Some teens needed a gentle prod to discover deodorant. Frankie needed someone to hold him down and force it on him.

"Shut the fuck up loser. You think I'm scared? I'm the one who stole ol' man Morrison's car wasn't I? While you sat crying in the bushes. You're the bitch."

I could see my brothers reply stung Frankie. I was shocked he didn't slug my brother because of it. I was also shocked by what Mikey had said; *he stole a car?*

"Ok, so here's how we settle this then. We all go. If none of us are bitches, then we *all* go and see if it's real or not. Kyle said he saw it with his own eyes. So either he's full of shit or he saw it."

That was Andrew. The voice of reason. He was the mature one of the group and even had his driver's license already. When he spoke the group listened.

So it was, on that July afternoon, I watched the boys walk away, heading to see if that little girl really did hide in the trees.

I felt hopeless. I felt scared. I wanted to run and tell my parents, to cry, to yell and beg Mikey to stay behind.

He looked back and saw my devastated face watching them. He jogged back and knelt down to look directly into my eyes and smiled.

"Jason. Listen buddy, don't tell mom, ok? I'll be back shortly and tell you what. When I get home, I'll ditch these douchebags and me and you will spend the night playing Nintendo together. Sound good?"

I let out a little sniff, but nodded. *That sounded great.* He squeezed my shoulder and turned, jogging back to catch up with the group. Then they disappeared around the corner and vanished from my life.

I sat on the front step for the next four hours, patiently waiting for my brother to return. I cradled the Nintendo controller I had retrieved, and watched as the sun dipped low and the streetlights burst into life.

My mom came out and let me know dinner was ready. When I said I would wait for Mikey, she replied he was probably off with his friends and to come inside.

I fell asleep that night in Mikey's room, sitting on his bean bag chair, still holding that controller.

2.

When I woke up the next day, I knew something was wrong.

When I entered the kitchen, my mom's face was red and puffy from hours of crying. My dad had a hand on her shoulder while he spoke to the two police officers. They were busy jotting down notes in their notepads.

When the adults spotted my entrance, their conversation stopped and my mom came to me right away and hugged me hard.

"Jason, can you please tell these officers what your brother told you yesterday?" My dad didn't sound too thrilled to have me there now.

I told them the whole conversation I had eaves dropped on. My dad's eyebrows went up when I mentioned Mikey stealing a car, but he didn't say anything.

Finally I got to the end and paused, tears spilling out.

"It's ok son," the taller officer said, "take your time. And don't be scared. You won't be in trouble for telling us the truth."

I looked searchingly at my mom, hoping for some sort of guidance. She met my eyes and smiled. That was all I needed.

"They went to find the girl that hides in the trees."

3.

The next few months were a painful blur. Funerals for Andrew, Kyle, Frankie and finally Mikey. I was numb. Eight years old and learning about mortality by sitting in a church listening to a pastor talk about God and how He had a plan for these young souls.

My parents lived life in a fog, making me meals but that was about it. The funerals were the only time I had seen mom not in her house coat since before Mikey disappeared.

It was years later, when I was twelve, before I ever found out some details about what happened. Or more accurately, what was found.

On the far side of town lies McConnell's Forest. Named after one of the founding fathers of our town, the forest covers thousands of acres of land, and comes right up to the highway. The town had built a very nice park area, hoping people would use the walking trails and the picnic benches, but the rumours that persisted about what lurked in the trees was enough to keep most away. The town didn't want to waste taxpayer dollars maintaining a place no one used, so the area became neglected and overrun with brush and weeds.

All of that combined to make it the perfect hangout spot for high school kids. They would head out there, parking in the gravel lot and walk in. They knew the cops wouldn't hassle anyone there, so they could drink, do drugs or hook up without fear of discovery.

That exact reasoning led to my brother and his group being found. Or parts of them, more precisely.

McConnell's Forest had been the site of the original town when the first group of European settlers arrived. They camped in the woods while clearing the land to build the permanent buildings. It took a few years before most people no longer camped, having built houses to live in. A decade later and the town was habitable and only the poorest people still camped instead of living in small houses.

The people camping were treated like scum and the history books were not so kind to this group. Sadly there was little respect shown towards the campers.

The urban legend said, that one night a few men who were drunk went to the outskirts of the camp, and began to assault the women. They would rip off their clothes, pull their hair and grope them against their will.

During this attack the men of the campsite fought back and eventually the drunk men left. The tale varies here. Some say the drunk men returned later that night in revenge, some say they returned a few days later or a few months later. No matter the case, it was discovered that a young girl, only ten years old, had disappeared, never to be seen again.

Now of course this was not typically worthwhile news. Except for the fact that in the ensuing years, McConnell's Forest played host to a number of spooky events, mysterious disappearances and gruesome discoveries.

Hikers reported seeing a young girl far ahead of them on the path, only to never catch up to her, never see her again. Some heard a child crying at night or a girl calling for her mom. Pets would go missing and only their collars would be found years later.

Over the three hundred years that the town had existed, at least a hundred people had been reported missing in the forest. The last missing hiker had occurred only four years ago. Someone reported that Karl Radler had not returned home after going for a weekend hike. His car was found parked in the gravel lot, keys in the ignition. His body was never found, nor was his backpack. The search and rescue team had called off the search when the K9 dog lost Karl's trail in the middle of a large clearing.

"Doesn't make any sense," the dog's handler said as they searched for any sign of the man.

All of this combined to create an urban legend that continued to grow in scope and in fright factor. It wasn't lost on me that Karl had gone missing not long after my brother and his friends had disappeared. I was a young boy with a curious mind and the 'unknown' intrigued me.

I started to search for answers to the questions I had about my brother's death. Mikey had been such a rock star in my mind. He was only sixteen when he died, but to me he always appeared so much older. The things he had introduced me to shaped my little brain and I was forever grateful for how great of a brother he had been. He let me watch horror movies with him that my parents wouldn't let me see. He showed me his nudie mags, gave me my first taste of beer and showed me how to sneak into the movie theatre for free. Now, none of this sounds great to an adult mind, but when you are eight years old its mind blowing.

I felt lost for a few years after he was buried. Now though, I wanted answers. I wanted to know what happened to my brother and his friends. A small part of me believed there was something lurking in McConnell's Forest, but the logical part of my pre-teen brain told me it was a bear or a cougar, not an urban legend come to life.

I dedicated many hours at the school library, searching Google for articles related to their disappearance and discovery. I was surprised when I finally got a solid hit from our local newspaper.

July 3, 2006

MISSING BOYS FOUND – FOUL PLAY SUSPECTED

The date and the headline made me stop and stare. I was transported back to that Monday night, sitting on the porch with the Nintendo controller.

I kept reading, doing my best to keep my emotions under control. I knew now why my parents had worked so hard to protect me from the details.

Authorities searching the area in McConnell's Forest, near the last known location of the group of missing boys, say they have found confirmed remains of all five. Early indications suggest that the boys were out in the area attempting to 'debunk' a local urban legend before they were reported missing. Autopsies will be performed to confirm cause of death. A spokesman for the county sheriff's office speaking on condition of anonymity says that the remains discovered were gruesome and suggest a violent attack occurred. While no complete bodies were located, enough parts of each boy were found, enabling parents and authorities to conclude that all were accounted for.

Local police ask the public to remain vigilant while out hiking, and to please stay away from the area currently as it is still an active and ongoing investigation.

The parents of the boys have asked for the public's understanding in this horrible time and to please respect their privacy as they cope.

I got up, went to the washroom and splashed my face with water.

My eyes were burning and I could feel the dam getting closer and closer

to bursting. *Not at the school library*, I thought. I had cried hundreds of

times since my brother died but I had made sure to never cry at school,

never in front of any of my classmates. I was already looked at with

distance. I was the kid whose brother died. I didn't also want to gain a

reputation as being unstable or a crier.

I went back and continued my search and stumbled on another

article from two days later.

July 5, 2006

AUTHORITIES CONFIRM ANIMAL ATTACK

Authorities have confirmed their earlier suspicions that an animal had attacked and

was considered responsible in the deaths of five local boys. The boys had been

witnessed heading into McConnell's Forest, attempting to 'debunk' an ongoing

local urban legend.

Jerry McKewn, spokesman for the county coroner, said that puncture wounds, bite marks and defensive wounds matched several previous cases of animal attacks in the same area.

"We spent many man hours on both the search and on determining what happened once we found the remains. We are satisfied with the findings and consider this case closed. Our deepest condolences to the families," Jerry stated to the gathered reporters.

Local police have contacted conservation officers, who have set up several traps in the area. The hope is to trap the suspect animal and recover more remains if possible.

There it was. In print. My brother had been attacked and devoured by some brute in the woods. All because they wanted to see if that stupid urban legend was real. This was the first time I had felt anger towards my brother since he died. Why? Why did he have to do something so stupid, so irresponsible and die?

I knew I should have considered it case closed. The authorities

had spoken and I should have just moved on. But he was my brother,

my best friend. I stopped searching for answers for the next few years.

Then on my fourteenth birthday I was reminded that maybe there

was something to that urban legend.

4.

I had started hanging around with Andrew's younger sister Vanessa, after his death. Nothing serious, just someone my age that I could talk openly to about losing a sibling. We kept our distance at school and made sure that no one caught on to us hanging out all the time. As we got older I realized I was falling into something resembling love. She was kind, compassionate and gave the best hugs. I didn't remember the exact moment it struck me, but one day it dawned on me that I wanted nothing more than to kiss her.

I was too shy, too scared to try anything, so I left it alone. I didn't want to lose my best friend by doing something stupid or unwanted.

On my fourteenth birthday, my parents woke me up with breakfast in bed. Then they told me that my friends had planned a fun afternoon before we would come back to the house for a BBQ, cake and my present.

I greedily ate and got ready, before heading over to my buddy Rod's place. When I arrived I was showered with confetti and then blasted with water balloons. After all of the laughter finally died down, I was told of the big plans for the day. We were going to go zip-lining!

I was blown away. I had always wanted to go and contrary to people's beliefs I was fine with McConnell's Forest. I wasn't going to not do something simply because it was located near the woods.

We piled into Rod's parents' mini-van, six of us squeezing in, and headed to the zip-line place. It was located about a mile from where they had found my brother, but I put that out of my mind and focused on enjoying myself.

As we pulled into the parking lot for the zip-line, two more cars pulled up beside us. I was so surprised to see all of my friends pile out.

Vanessa was one of the first ones out and gave me the biggest smile. I felt my insides quiver and shake.

"HAPPY BIRTHDAY!"

The entire group yelled out and then they all jumped on me, yelling and trying to scruff up my hair.

Once the mass of kids moved off of me I looked around at everyone with joy.

"Thank you all for coming," I said and we proceeded to the small shack to get set up to have fun.

*

Deep within McConnell's Forest she stirred. The sun couldn't penetrate the canopy of branches in the old woods. In the darkness below a thick redwood, she skipped, her tattered dress bouncing and swishing with her movements. She smiled, thinking about the joy she was sure to have soon. Her lips were cracked and blistered, the teeth dark and decayed.

"Come my friends," she sung, leaving her sleeping hole. Ahead

were her playthings, and she had waited oh so long to have a play date.

5.

I couldn't picture a more magical birthday afternoon if I tried.

Gavin had done such a fantastic job of inviting my friends and arranging

for the zip-line to be closed to the public. We had free range of the

entire area.

The zip-line place was more of a fun park. It also included mini-

golf, a go-cart area and a small man-made river where you could float

around the edge of the park on inner tubes.

I must have done the zip-line twenty times, as each time I got in

line everyone chanted, "Birthday boy to the front of the line!"

I would then be pushed and pulled to the front of the line and

would take another zip down.

The part though that I enjoyed the most was floating on the inner

tubes. Why? Because I was able to spend some 'close' quality time

with Vanessa. In such a big group we were able to easily steal glances

at each other and share quick smiles. It was during the day that it dawned on me that Vanessa was looking at me *differently*. She was no longer looking at me like her friend Jason. She was looking at me with *something* more than friendliness. Every time our inner tubes bumped my stomach flipped or flopped.

"Ok gang, thirty minutes and then we gotta go!"

Rod's mom yelled out and the group gave out a collective groan of disappointment.

"Inner tubes one more time?" I asked Vanessa hopefully.

"I was hoping you would ask," she replied, smiling at me coyly.

I helped her get onto her inner tube, savoring the feeling of her soft hand in mine. I climbed onto my floating seat and we were off, slowly floating around the perimeter.

We were laughing and splashing water at each other, having a great time. Then something changed. It was though my color TV suddenly reverted to black and white. I could see Vanessa laughing and splashing, but all around her the sky darkened and the trees grew menacing.

I felt a cold shiver pass through my body and I looked beyond Vanessa, to the edge of the woods. That's when I saw him.

Mikey.

He was standing there watching me, body half hidden by a thick tree. He was leaning out to see us, which exposed some of the right side of his body. His arm was missing from the elbow down, shredded skin hanging below loosely. His face had deep gouge marks across it, exposing the bone below.

When we made eye contact his face spread into a sickly grin. Because of the damage done to his cheek and jaw, as the smile spread his face looked like a constrictor beginning to swallow a larger victim.

I couldn't look away. His eyes burned deep into me, causing physical pain. *Mikey.* Then I felt the rain begin to fall, cascading from the sky. I could hear someone yelling. Then the sky cleared, my vision returned into color and Mikey was gone.

Vanessa was yelling at me as she kept splashing me with water.

"Earth to Jason? Hello?" She quipped as she rapidly doused with me with water. It wasn't raining on me, it had been her all along.

"Sorry, I thought I saw something," I mumbled before splashing her back. I didn't want her to suspect anything odd or weird. I would spend some time replaying the events later. For now I was going to enjoy my day.

*

We wrapped up at the zip-line, thanked all of the fantastic staff and then piled back into the cars. Then we drove over to my house for a fantastic birthday BBQ. It was the best way to end an already amazing day. I felt blessed to have so many friends who truly cared about me. I knew that the stigma of having a brother die can be tough to kick in such a small town, so I was thankful that they all saw through that.

As the day turned into night and the sun dipped low, the moon rising high, we all stayed out in our backyard. My parents had always prided themselves on our backyard. It was large, with lots of grass, a games place where some people were playing horse shoes, and a large wooden swing that could fit four people.

I was sitting on it alone, taking a moment to wind down from the excitement of the day. I laid my head back and closed my eyes, letting my body relax, when I felt someone sit down beside me on the bench. The first thought through my mind was; *please don't be Mikey*.

I opened my eyes and turned, relieved to see Vanessa sitting there instead of my dead brother.

"Hey," I said, getting her attention.

"Oh hey, sorry wasn't trying to interrupt your nap," she replied jokingly.

"Nah, I wasn't napping. I had fun today."

"Me too," she replied staring at me deeply.

I was about to ask her if something was wrong when she leaned in quickly and kissed me deeply. I felt the intensity of her kiss, the passion flow through her lips and when her tongue found mine I officially landed on cloud nine.

Then we both heard it. Our entire group of gathered friends began to *ooh* and *awe*. We had been spotted.

We broke away sheepishly, but Vanessa kept her hand on my thigh. I knew I looked like an underage drunk, but I didn't care. My entire life had just been made.

"Nice," Gavin said as he strode up and slapped my shoulder. "Happy birthday dude. And glad to see you and Vanessa can stop hiding your feelings." He chuckled as he walked away. Apparently we hadn't been that stealthy after all.

"Thank you," I said to Vanessa quietly and squeezed her hand on my thigh. She looked over and smiled at me warmly. I was glad to see that my lack of experience with kissing hadn't turned her off from me, her eyes glowing when she smiled.

"I have to get going soon. Happy birthday Jason. You deserve to be happy."

We stood up and we hugged, but decided not to kiss again, knowing the entire group was staring intently at us now.

It didn't take long after Vanessa was picked up by her parents that the rest of my friends all hitched rides back to their houses. Walking at night had become a thing of the past since my brother and his friends had met their demise.

I thanked my parents for such a fantastic day and said I was going to head to bed.

"Don't you want your gift?" My dad asked as I started up the stairs to my room.

"Wasn't the zip-line and BBQ my gift?"

"Nope. Here," he said handing me a box.

I opened the flaps and couldn't believe what I was looking at.

"Is this…?" I was trying to hold it together.

"Yup. It's his. We found it in the garage a few months back and thought you might want it." My mom spoke as she walked over to me.

I pulled the game console out of the box and looked it over. Mikey's Nintendo. I couldn't believe it. I hadn't seen it since the morning after he walked away with his friends. My parents had packed his belongings up quickly after he was found. I had never set foot in his empty room since.

"Thank you. This is… this is maybe the best thing you have ever given me."

I hugged them both and then ran up to my room.

That night I fell asleep playing Excite Bike, forgetting all about what I had spotted at the zip-line park.

6.

A scratching noise woke me up sometime during the night.

It was faint but it didn't stop. I stood up and looked at my window but saw it wasn't coming from there.

I left my room and stopped in the upstairs landing, trying to get a location of where it was coming from.

The scratching continued and I whirled around trying to pinpoint the direction. Then it hit me.

Mikey's room.

The scratching was coming from a room that hadn't been opened in almost a decade.

I slowly walked over to the door and dropped to the floor trying to look underneath it. There was just enough space that I could see into the room a little bit. If something or someone was in the room, they would need to be standing at the door for me to know they were in there.

"*Jason*," a gravelled voice whispered, followed by more

scratching.

I felt the contents of my stomach move into my throat.

"*Jason, let me out*," the voice whispered. A stench of rotting meat

and garbage assailed my nostrils and I pulled away from the door.

There was no mistaking the voice. That was my brother. But

how?

I knelt back down.

"Mikey? Is that you?"

I tried to be quiet, not wanting my parents to be disturbed or to

stumble out onto this scene.

"*Jason. Please help, let me out*," the voice pleaded.

I moved my face closer and thought for a brief moment that I

could see a darkened object where once there had been nothing.

"Mikey?" I asked again.

Then I saw a flash of movement and a long, decayed finger with a razor sharp fingernail lashed out and sliced my cheek.

I rolled away in agony and howled. My cheek had burst open and blood was splashing over my hands and forearms, spraying the hallway. My mom and dad rushed from their room, finding me trying to stem the flow of blood.

"Oh my god," my dad yelled out before rushing into the bathroom and retrieving a towel. He held it up to my face, trying to stop the bleeding.

"Jason, what happened?" he asked as he pulled the towel away to look at the damage. "Jesus Christ. He's gonna need stitches. Go start the car and I will get him down there," my dad said to my mom, who didn't wait and turned, heading down the stairs.

"Easy kiddo. Let's go, take the steps slowly. One at a time."

We made our way down to the car and we headed off to the hospital. As we pulled away from the house I saw a dark silhouette in the window of Mikey's room.

7.

Ten stitches later and I was all sewn up. It wasn't lost on me that the spot I was given stitches matched one of the gashes I had spotted on Mikey's face in the woods.

I had fudged the truth a bit to my parents when they asked what I was doing. I told them I had heard a noise and thought maybe an animal had gotten somehow. Because of the lie I was rewarded by also receiving a rabies shot, a tetanus shot and a stern scolding by the attending physician.

When we got home my dad decided it was worth investigating the room, to see if something had somehow found its way in.

"Better to be safe than sorry," he said as we went to Mikey's door. My mom refused to be a part of the investigation. She stayed downstairs, making herself some coffee.

Standing at the door with my dad, I was filled with anxiety and dread.

What if something was behind that door?

My dad didn't have any reservations though, and before I could attempt to stop him and tell him my worries, he unlocked the door and pushed it open.

We were hit by the overwhelming smell of stale air and decade old dust. He reached his hand tentatively into the room, his fingers searching for a brief second before finding the light switch and then the room was illuminated before us.

"Surprised the bulb still works," he mentioned as he entered the room.

The room was bare. My parents had stripped it clean of all items and furniture before the funeral and since then the only inhabitant had been the growing layer of dust on the floor.

My dad checked the window and it wouldn't budge. Nothing had entered or exited through there recently. He then checked the corners, then the ceiling and finally opened the closet and inspected in there.

Nothing.

"Not sure what to say Jason. Nothing's been in here recently. Are you sure you're ok? We can set up an appointment with the counsellor if you need to talk to someone."

My dad was amazing and had never judged me for wanting to see a counsellor once. But I knew what I had heard, what I had saw and I had ten stitches throbbing on my face to prove I wasn't losing my mind.

"No, I'm fine. Thanks though."

"Did your cheek maybe get sliced on the bottom of the door?"

I shook my head. That wasn't an option. We turned to leave the room when I spotted a discrepancy on the floor. I crouched down to look and my dad followed.

"What's that?" He asked.

I felt my blood run cold as my dad touched the floor and felt the odd marks.

"Scratch marks," I replied before quickly leaving the room.

8.

I stayed distant from my friends the next few days. It was easy in the summer. I didn't have to run into them every day at school and if I didn't want to go anywhere I didn't have to.

My parents left me alone, asking if I was ok and offering to give me a ride anywhere. I politely declined.

I was texting a bunch with Vanessa and finally after she poked and prodded enough I told her that I needed to talk to her, and asked if she could come by. She replied that her mom could bring her over in a few hours.

So I sat and waited, kept myself occupied until I heard the doorbell ring.

I was so happy to see her. The darkness that had been clinging to my heart was temporarily abated.

I had sent her a few pics of my face with the stitches, but this was the first time she had seen it in person.

"Oh Jason," she said as she stepped closer in concern.

She gently touched my cheek and stroked the area by the stitches with the softness of her finger tips.

My mom and dad both stood and stared with wide eyes. I had been so lost in the oblivion of her and her touch that I failed to register them coming to see who was at the door.

"Ahem," my dad cleared his throat and I jumped.

"Sorry dad, didn't even see you guys there," I meekly replied.

"Hello Vanessa," my mom said, face spread wide in the biggest smile I had seen on her in some time.

"Hey," Vanessa shyly replied, embarrassed by the awkward situation.

"So… are you two… like… a thing?" I hadn't heard my dad stumble through a sentence like that in some time and it almost caused me to chuckle.

"I think so," Vanessa replied and stepped closer, grabbing my hand.

My eyes went wide. *We were a thing?* My heart was now tap dancing against my lung.

"Well that's great news. Small change then. If Vanessa is over we expect your door to be open," my dad said, trying to speak with authority.

I nodded in understanding.

"And," my mom piped up, "If you are going to stay the night, your parents need to know you are a thing first. If they say you can't stay over, then you both have to follow our rules. We're comfortable with you staying over. You have before. We know you're both responsible. If Vanessa is going to sleep in your room Jason, then we can bring the spare mattress up from the basement. And the door stays open."

I was blown away. My parents had always been, what I considered, cool parents. This now confirmed it for me.

"Understood," I replied. My parents looked over at Vanessa.

"Understood. I haven't told my parents yet but I will. I thought Jason wanted to discuss *us* actually."

My parents, sensing a moment, let us be, and we retreated to the sanctity of my room.

We sat and were quiet for some time. Finally I built up my courage and spoke.

"Vanessa. I don't know where to start but I'm just going to. Let me tell you what's happened and then maybe we can figure this out."

She nodded and sat quietly, legs crossed, hair pulled back. I was awestruck by her beauty. It took her kissing me at my birthday party to pull back all of those feelings I had buried.

I filled her in. I started at the zip-line park, seeing Mikey, describing the color shift and the rain. Then I told her about that night. The scratching, the voice and then what I saw before my face was ripped open. To her credit she remained silent, stoic even. Occasionally her eyebrows went up or kinked, as she processed what I was saying. When I finally finished with telling her about feeling the scratch marks on the floor, I sat back and exhaled. A weight had been lifted from my chest, as though the darkness had been filled with helium.

"So if you think I'm crazy, and I don't blame you, just please tell me. And as much as it would hurt, we don't have to keep being *us*, if that has scared you."

I almost burst out crying saying those words.

Vanessa moved close and took my hands in hers. She leaned in and gave me a soft kiss on my lips and then embraced me in a deep hug. I broke down and sobbed into her shoulder.

"Thanks," I said as I pulled away and wiped my eyes. "I needed to get that off my chest."

Vanessa's face had changed though.

"What is it?"

"I've had an experience too."

9.

I listened quietly now to Vanessa. I was there for her, as she had just been for me.

"It was last week. I finished babysitting for Mr. and Mrs. Aslow. My mom was running late so I decided I would just walk until she arrived. I mean, I know we try not to be out after dark or near the woods at least, but it was four in the morning. I felt bad having my mom have to come. So I figured if I saved her some time and she could get back home faster, it would be helpful."

She glanced up at me before continuing.

"I was walking away from the house, down the street. I knew my mom would come up the highway before turning off towards the Aslow's, so I was going to walk that way while making sure to stay on the opposite side of McConnell's Forest. I figured if something made a noise or whatever I could just turn around and go back to the Aslow's. There was just enough morning light that I could see something ahead of me. It was moving around in the middle of a tree down the road. I know I should have just stopped and turned around, but I was curious. I felt drawn to it, Jason. Like you described; I felt like Andrew was trying to communicate or something. So I stayed on the opposite side and kept walking. When I got near I was able to make out what it was."

Vanessa stopped talking and all I could hear was my heart pounding in my chest. I looked down to see if I could physically see it pushing out.

"Jason. It was a girl's dress. A fucking girl's dress caught in a tree blowing around in the wind. But there wasn't any wind, Jason. There wasn't any wind. Then I felt a chill. It was so cold, all of my skin crawled and the hairs on my arms stood on end. I couldn't take my eyes off the dress. As I got directly across from it I saw that most of the dress was stained red. Jason, it was covered in blood. I bolted. I couldn't help it. I was scared so I ran, I ran as fast as I could."

Vanessa started crying so I moved beside her and comforted her as she had me. I thought her story was over, but to my dismay it wasn't.

"Jason, as I ran, something started chasing me. I looked back a few times, but couldn't see anything at first. Then I caught movement in the trees. Something black was moving through the trees just beyond the ditch. I couldn't see what it was, but I knew it was evil. I saw headlights ahead and knew it was my mom. I tried to run faster but I couldn't move, and I heard the thing getting closer. Then it started talking. It was a young girl's voice but the voice sounded ancient. The voice just said my name over and over. Finally my mom pulled up and I jumped in. I didn't tell her what I saw or why I was running. She just assumed it was because I was scared of the dark. When she turned around to leave I looked back. Nothing was there. The dress was gone."

I hugged her as hard as I could and wiped her tears away with my hand.

We didn't say anything else that night. We just lay beside each other before falling asleep. When my mom came up to ask if Vanessa was sleeping over she found us sound asleep on my bed. She covered us in my blanket before going downstairs and calling Vanessa's mom.

10

When we woke up we made a plan.

We had to get to the bottom of this. This thing, this demon girl or whatever it was, had killed too many. It was holding our town hostage. Whether it was a real thing, or just simply an urban legend, we had to find out the truth and deal with it.

"We need to get some of our friends to help us. I know Gavin will. We can probably get Mason and David. What about on your side?"

I knew those three would help no question. Mason and David were solid guys, my best friends since childhood. Mason was introspective. Even though he was only fourteen he would remove his glasses and wipe them off while looking off in the distance. A deep thinker. David was our resident movie expert. I didn't know anyone who had watched more horror flicks than David. Both of them were on the soccer team. Gavin, well Gavin was my brother from another mother. He was always there to pick me up when I was down. When I was eight and fell off the swings, chipping my tooth, he had even accompanied me to the dentist to make sure I was ok. I had such a solid, dependable group of friends. I was truly lucky.

"I think I can get Sarah and probably Jen."

Perfect, I thought.

Both Sarah and Jen ran track at our school. The more people we could get that were fast and not afraid the better. Sarah was also taller than every other girl in our school. She constantly hated being asked if she played basketball, but would use her height as an advantage every chance she got.

The seven of us would make for a strong group to get to the bottom of whatever was happening out at McConnell's Forest.

Vanessa and I spent the next few minutes texting our friends, inviting them over to my place for lunch. We didn't tell them details, just that we wanted to discuss something with them.

Not surprisingly all three of my friends replied with the same text back; *"She's preggo isn't she?"*

Sarah and Jen both replied with a different version;

"You're not pregnant are you?"

"Wow our friends are so funny," I said as I chuckled, feeling uneasy even thinking about the topic of getting Vanessa pregnant. I mean, sure I was fourteen and had normal teenage urges, but this was all so new and exciting. I wasn't even thinking that far ahead.

While we waited for our friends to arrive, we started to come up with our cover to tell our parents. We would need to all have the same story and none of us could risk any discrepancy. One small difference and we knew one of our parents would sniff it out.

"I'm stumped Vanessa. What can we possibly tell all of our parents that would allow us to camp out overnight in McConnell's Forest?"

We bandied about a few ideas before settling on the oldest and most commonly used teenage lie there was. We would tell each set of parents we were all spending the weekend over at someone else's house.

I called my friend Rod to see if he would be our cover. Rod was a massive stoner and spent all of his time getting high and playing video games. He agreed without even asking what we were planning on really doing. He didn't care. All he asked was for each of us to pay him $10.

When the others finally arrived, I felt confident. I needed to get to the bottom of this. I wanted closure; for me, for Vanessa, for Mikey and for the town. We wanted our freedom back and we were determined to get it.

Well, the two of us were.

The rest of the invited were not receptive at all.

"Dude. Seriously. You want us to do what?" Gavin asked.

"Like camp-out, camp-out? Spend the night there and everything?" Sarah was less than enthused with the prospect of staying in that forest, in the dark, in a tent.

"Look guys. I know this doesn't mean as much to you as it does for Jason and I," Vanessa said, pleading her case, "But we need to get to the bottom of this. Not just for us, but for everyone in this town. Generations of people have lived in fear and it's time it stopped."

The five looked at each other, searching for a signal or someone to take a stand against doing this. But when none came, we all collectively nodded. It was settled. The seven of us would head to McConnell's Forest.

The seven of us were going to confront the girl who hid in the trees.

11.

All of our parents gave us permission to stay at Rod's for the weekend without even a second thought. This would let us camp both Friday and Saturday night if needed. We made a trip to the food market and stocked up on supplies. We packed the tents and supplies into my parents van and my mom gave us a ride over to Rod's. Gavin had got his parents to give him, Mason and David a ride, so all seven of us arrived together. It would be a thirty minute hike from Rod's place to the base of the path that led deep into McConnell's Forest. This was also the path where the hiker Karl was last seen alive.

We were all quiet as we made the trek to the forest. Contemplating what was to come? Hard to say. I thought about two things; the first was, was there truth to the urban legend? The second was how fantastic Vanessa's rear looked in front of me in her black tights.

When we all arrived at the gravel parking lot before the start of the path, we all stopped and drank from our water bottles, taking a minute to steady our nerves.

"Ok, here we go," I said, trying to sound brave.

"Wait," Gavin piped up. "Maybe we should say a prayer before we go?"

If I had any water left in my mouth, I would have spit it out. Gavin was the furthest thing from religious.

"Uh, sure," I responded.

"Dear Lord," Gavin started, and I saw that everyone had bowed their heads, so I followed suit.

"Please Lord, protect us from the forest. And please Lord, if you can, make sure Sarah, Jen and Vanessa keep wearing those fantastic tights. Their asses looks so amazing, I know a few tents are being pitched already. OW!"

Vanessa and Jen slugged him in each shoulder simultaneously and Gavin dropped his back pack to the ground frantically rubbing his shoulders.

The rest of us burst out laughing.

"Ok, enough jokes. Let's go. Stay close. We really don't know what's happening, so let's make sure if it is an animal, none of us become a victim."

We then left the lot, travelling in single file, myself at the front, followed by Vanessa, Sarah, Jen, Mason, David and Gavin at the back. As the forest welcomed us, I noticed a tiny hint of something in the air.

Rotting meat and decay.

12.

Two hours into the journey and we finally all decided it was time to take a break and have an afternoon snack. We still had about four hours of daylight left and I wanted to use another two hours to hike further into the forest. There was a lake I wanted to reach so we could camp beside it. I had been there once before many years ago, when Mikey was alive and I remembered it had a very nice sandy beach.

I figured at the least, even if we struck out finding the source of the urban legend, we could enjoy the beach and have a good weekend of camping and swimming. I knew Gavin wouldn't mind if these girls were frolicking in their bikinis.

I filled the group in on where I wanted us to hike to and all were in agreement. The day was gorgeous. Sunny, barely any clouds in the sky, but we were treated to a slight breeze that kept the heat from becoming too much. The other six were also all in great shape from their various sports, so no one was complaining about how awful it was to hike this far or bitching about the heat. We all knew why we were here and it was refreshing to just hike and chat as though we were on a casual stroll through the woods.

Then after another few hours we all felt the change in the air. That smoothly sweet change when you get close to a large body of water on a hot day. The wind became damp, the trees fluttered a bit more and we could hear more birds chirping.

We had arrived.

It was even better than I remembered.

There was a large area designated for tents, as evidenced by the crudely constructed rock fire pits set around the space. Before them was a long, lush sandy beach that disappeared into some of the bluest water we had laid our eyes on. It was a hidden paradise in the middle of a deeply troubled nightmare. McConnell's Forest had its share of secrets, but this was one I was glad it gave up.

We spent some time setting up and arranging the tents. We had the three girls staying in one tent, which we placed in the middle. Then on either side we set up a tent for us boys. Me and Gavin were going to share one and Mason and David the other. Once all three were up and operational, we scouted the area for firewood.

"Hey guys! Holy shit balls! Come check this out."

It was Mason. We all rushed in the direction he had been searching, each of us conjuring up a picture in our mind of some horribly gruesome discovery.

When we found him, what we spotted was the furthest from gruesome. Mason had stumbled on an old picnic table, discarded in the bushes.

"Help me bring this over to the tents. This will be perfect for eating at."

I grabbed one corner while Gavin and David grabbed one each as well. Then the four of us lugged the old, heavy, wooden picnic table from the undergrowth and over to the campsite.

"Why would someone discard this?" Sarah asked.

It took us a few seconds to see why.

The entire table top was covered in carvings from various people over the years. None of them were easy to read.

SHE'S WATCHING read one.

THE TREES ARE SPYING, BEWARE! Read another.

They kept going. I read a few more before deciding we didn't need to continue, so went and grabbed a towel from my bag and laid it down, covering them all up.

"Thank you," Vanessa said as she came over and took my hand.

We still had a few hours of sunlight left, so we decided to enjoy the beach and get in a swim. Gavin, to my surprise, said he was tired and wanted a nap. I figured he would be the first one in the water, getting waist deep as quickly as he could to hide his erection as the girls tanned on the sand.

After we were done swimming we all dried off around the fire that David had started and prepared some dinner. *If we weren't out here looking for a dead ghost-girl this would be one of the best weekends of my life,* I thought.

After dinner was finished and we had cleaned up, we all sat around the camp fire just enjoying each other's company. Vanessa snuggled up beside me and the warmth that she gave me was only amplified by the feeling of peace I had, by being able to share our affections publicly.

As the sun set, the sky blazed crimson and a lone loon called out from the lake. A mild breeze was enough to create a gentle rhythm of waves lapping the shore and I found myself hypnotized by the groove of nature. *This was where I was meant to be,* I thought, *surrounded by this group, in this place.*

In reality we were hours away from horror. From our group being ripped apart and things changing forever. For now though, I squeezed Vanessa's hand and kissed her forehead, wishing the fire would never burn out and that we would never grow up.

13.

"Jason you need to get out here."

Gavin's voice ripped me from my sleep and I hurriedly made my way out of the tent. It was pitch black out so it took a minute for my eyes to adjust and let the light of the moon illuminate the gathered group.

That's when I noticed we were one short.

"Where's Jen?" I asked, not wanting an answer.

"She went to go pee," Sarah said, visibly shaking. Vanessa wrapped an arm around her, pulling her close.

"She left to go and I fell back asleep. Then a little girl woke me up. She said don't worry, it's just a dream. She said Jen tasted delicious and she couldn't wait to see how I tasted. I woke up when I felt her long finger nail slicing my leg. When I opened my eyes it was just me and Vanessa, but look," she said lifting her leg out in front of her to show us.

Her black tights had a long cut down the side of her thigh. Behind it I could see a sizeable cut in her leg and dried blood around it.

"Where's Jen?" Sarah asked and then burst out crying, Vanessa holding her close.

I turned to Gavin, Mason and David. They all looked frightened and I assumed I looked the same.

"Ok boys. We need to do a search. Let's split into two groups and try and find her. Me and Gav and you two. Don't let each other out of your sights. We meet back here in thirty minutes, unless someone finds Jen before. Vanessa, you and Sarah stay here in case she comes back. Maybe she's just lost."

Everyone nodded in agreement. David went over and got the fire going again, creating some much welcomed warmth. Vanessa led Sarah over to the fire to warm them up.

"Guys, we don't really have any weapons to defend ourselves with?"

Mason sheepishly spoke up, but we all realized he was right.

"Fuck." David's response summed up what we were all thinking.

I went and searched the area behind the tents and found a few baseball bat sized branches.

"Guess this will do," I said, handing one to Vanessa and the other to David and Mason. I went back and found two more, keeping one for myself and giving the other to Gavin.

"Ok, thirty minutes. Wish us luck." I quickly gave Vanessa a kiss and squeezed Sarah's shoulder.

"Don't worry Sarah. We'll find her."

We did.

14.

David and Mason kept close as they trudged off in the direction Sarah had thought Jen had went. Neither spoke, both focused on looking for any sign of Jen.

David had decided that they would limit the use of their flashlight.

"Look, in horror films, a flashlight is a beacon. It tells stuff out there exactly where we are. I don't want any fucking monster in the woods to know right where the fuck I am. Sound good?"

Mason was fine with that. Even though the trees were thick, they found that the moon was able to light the way sufficiently.

As the two were walking, Mason grabbed David's arm and gave it a frantic tug, causing David to stop. Looking at Mason, he saw his friend was staring off to their right and pointing.

David followed Mason's hand, seeing a dark figure off in the trees. His world grew hazy as he came close to passing out from fear.

"What the fuck is that," he whispered to Mason. Mason was breathing in short gasps, struggling to process the thing before them.

"David. Mason. Come. I will show you the way to your friend." The voice was deep and the accent hinted that this thing was very old.

The cloaked figure turned and began to walk away, deeper into the trees.

"Dude are we really going to follow that fucking thing?" David asked.

"It said it knows where Jen is. Shouldn't we? Or should we holler for Jason and Gavin to come and we all go?"

The two didn't know what to do. Then the decision was made for them. As they stood there trying to decide what to do a cackle of laughter pierced the blackness of the air. They turned and saw the figure had returned, this time accompanied by a small girl. She was wearing a full length, white dress that was adorned with frilly lace on each shoulder and through the neck.

"*Come, please*?" She asked, her voice so tender and sweet it would make even the hardest heart soften.

As though compelled forward by a hand pushing them from behind, Mason and David walked off the path and into the darkness before them.

15.

"Is that a light through the trees?"

Gavin asked the question quietly, as they searched for Jen. It had been fifteen minutes already and Jason was beginning to feel hopeless in their efforts.

"I think it is. That freaks me the fuck out," I replied. "Gav. I'm scared. I really am. Maybe we should've stayed home."

"Nope. I'm not having that dude. Something horrible happened to Mikey and his friends. You have to live with that every damn day. We are going to get to the bottom of this. One way or the other. It's either a bear or a ghost. We *need* to do this."

So we set off towards a light deep in McConnell's Forest. The closer we got the more I was thinking about previous hikers and campers. How many of them had spotted a light in the woods, only to never be seen again?

It became apparent that the light was actually a campfire. When we were near enough to see what it was, we were also able to make out that there were people sitting around it. Their backs were to us, but clear enough, we could see their shapes sitting on a log in front of a fire.

"What the fuck? Who the fuck's out here?" Gavin kept his voice low but it was anything but steady. I respected him to no end at that moment. For supporting me and for sacking up and not turning tail and running.

"Let's move slowly and make our way around to the front yeah? I don't know if it's the shadows playing tricks on my eyes, but I think I recognize the one in the middle," I said as we started to move.

As we made a slow arc around the perimeter, I knew my eyes were not lying. The one in the middle was my brother Mikey. I was pretty sure the one beside him was Andrew. My guts seized tight and I had to pause, waiting for the ferocious pain in my abdomen to subside.

Gavin didn't hear me stop, so he continued ahead. When I felt confident I was able to continue on, I started to move again, but before I had even made it ten feet I bumped into Gavin who was standing now, staring at the group. He was rock solid.

"Gavin, you ok?"

I stood beside him and saw he was wide-eyed.

"Jesus-fucking-Christ-what-the-fuck-are-those?" He tumbled out, now beginning to violently tremble.

I turned to see what he was looking at and felt my feet root hard to the forest floor.

It was the group of kids who had died that day. There was Mikey and Andrew and the rest.

But it wasn't exactly them. Instead of faces, each body had a massive horn protruding from their heads. Two of them had more than one horn. They had no eyes, no noses, no mouths. Instead it was covered with one long, thick horn, as though they had merged with a rhinoceros.

Gavin began now to stutter and a thick, red mucous-blood like fluid spurted and sputtered from his lips. His arms were flailing and flapping as he convulsed. I grabbed him tight not wanting him to fall. As I did that, I missed spotting the movement from the group around the fire. As I held Gavin, I suddenly heard pounding foot falls and I looked over at the last moment, before Andrew made contact and impaled Gavin through the stomach with the protruding spur.

Gavin made a pained noise as he was thrust out of my arms and thrown through the air. Andrew never stopped running though. He was immediately on top of Gavin and began to gore him and drive his face-horn into my friend. I heard more movement and looking back at the group saw that they were all now starting to walk towards me. I turned, dropped my 'weapon' and fled through the thickening woods, not realizing I was running in the wrong direction from camp. All I could think about was the sounds Gavin was making as I left him further and further behind.

16

Mason and David followed the girl and the cloaked figure through the forest before they entered a clearing. It wasn't until they had stopped walking that they realized a camp fire was burning in the centre of the space.

David was transfixed. Off to the right was a large, upright piano made entirely of bones. He could see that the keys were tiny skulls. The cloaked figure was now sat in front of it, playing a slow, sorrow-filled funeral dirge. As the figure played, the little girl danced lightly around the clearing, her feet appearing to not make contact with the ground.

Mason tapped David's shoulder and pointed at the fire. David looked away from the macabre ballet to see what had snagged Mason's attention.

Everyone who lived in the town knew exactly what Karl Radler looked like. He may have been missing and presumed dead for over a decade now, but so many articles and internet pieces had been devoted to him that his face was easily recognized by all.

Standing in the middle of the fire was Karl Radler, the missing hiker, who was greedily eating his own hands.

"What... the... actual... fuck..." David said.

As the flames grew higher around the man, the piano music grew in volume. Still the girl danced, her dress flowing around her as though caught in some unseen breeze.

"*Come, handsome boy. Come dance with this devil,*" she said as she took David by his hands. He couldn't stop himself. Now all he heard was the piano and all he saw was her eyes. They moved together in tiny circles, floating across the grass, as Mason watched on with shock.

The girl pulled David in close, so that now her head was beside his, her decayed skin scraping his face. She licked his ear, leaving a dripping trail of saliva behind before giggling. As they swooped around the area once again, picking up speed as the music went into double time, she breathed sweetly in his ear and then whispered to him;

"Underneath this moon my evil lips make contact,

For tonight is your last night on this earth.

I taste your blood and suck on your release sir,

For tonight is the night of my rebirth."

Then David screamed in agony as he held up two bloody stumps. Unbeknownst to him, the demonical girl had removed his fingers as they danced. Howling, he fell to his knees. Then he was tackled by Karl Radler, who began to feast on his amputated hands.

The sight of Karl's attack on David broke Mason free from his stupor. He rushed forward, but only made it a few feet before Jen stepped before him from the shadows and he fell backwards.

Her insides had been disembowelled, her organs missing from her stomach. He scrambled backwards as Jen hopped towards him, using her own intestines as a skipping rope.

It was then that he noticed she was missing her lower jaw, her tongue hanging freely below, wiggling back and forth towards him.

"Please, please, I don't want to die," he begged as he kept back-pedalling.

"*Aww. Sugar and spice and everything nice,*" the girl said from behind him. Mason abruptly turned to see the girl standing before him.

"Please. Please, whatever you want. I don't want to die," Mason begged as he bawled tears of deep fear.

"*You are in a mortal body on a mortal plane. Come, join me over here. Feed until full. Lust until satiated. I am the gate-keeper to your wildest desires. All you have to do is say the words and you can live in these trees for eternity, never wanting or needing for nothing.*"

As she spoke she seductively walked two of her fingers up from Mason's belt to the base of his chin, which he followed with his eyes. When she finished she tipped his chin up and they locked eyes.

Her words had been spoken in such a sing-song manner and had matched the eerie music from the piano so perfectly, Mason never felt

Jen wrap her intestines around his neck until it was too late. When she started squeezing tight, Mason smiled, feeling the fear drip from his body. Looking down he saw that the feeling wasn't fear dripping but his innards.

The girl cackled out loud as his organs spilled out and Mason began to scream. The last thing Mason ever saw was the dead hiker Karl, attacking and devouring his insides as Jen squeezed the intestines tighter.

17.

I ran for god only knows how long. Seeing my best friend Gavin murdered like that made my feet move without consulting my brain. I knew better. McConnell's Forest wasn't something I was unfamiliar with. To just run away deeper into *these* woods was stupid personified.

But here I was now. Lost.

I needed to get back to Vanessa and Sarah. Oh god! Vanessa. What if they have been attacked?

I frantically turned around in a circle, trying to make out anything that could point me in the right direction. Not surprisingly, everything was the same. I was surrounded by darkness and trees.

"Jason... Jason..." the sweet song of a child's voice pierced the black atmosphere.

I whirled around, trying to locate the source.

"Your brother put up such a fight. I could see you in his eyes. He so desperately wanted to live, to come back to you. Oh well. His heart was still beating while I swallowed it."

The voice had moved closer. I turned quickly to my left and spotted the ghost in the fog.

"Come face me," I boldly said. The courage I felt now came from an unknown place. I was scared deep down inside but felt emboldened by her talk of killing Mikey. I couldn't save him, but I wasn't going to let Vanessa die. Not tonight.

"Silly sapling. You think you have any chance at all against me?" She threw her head back and let out a laugh that was closer to a howl. It was so shrill that it caused me to cover my ears with my hands.

"We came to stop you. We're sick of living our lives in fear. What can we do to make you leave?"

The girl stopped laughing suddenly, as though shocked someone was talking *to* her not *at* her.

"*Sweet boy. Nothing can make me leave. I am cursed to be here forever more.*" She turned from me and I realized she was now weeping.

"I'm sorry someone hurt you. I truly am. If I was alive, back then, I would have tried to stop those men."

The girl turned back to me, and I could see just how young she was when she was alive. I didn't think she was any older than ten.

"May I ask your name?" I took a few steps towards her, but halted when she looked up. She may have once been a little girl, but it was obvious what now resided within her was pure evil.

"*I had a name once,*" she said as she took a step towards me, "*but I have long since forgotten it. The only way to break the curse and set me free is to say my name while casting off the spell. So as you can see, I can never leave.*"

I didn't know what to say. I was stunned to think I was having a conversation with *the* urban legend of McConnell's Forest. But more so, I felt horrible for this poor little girl, trapped here.

"No one has ever spoken to me like you have. I have let my guard down. I will make you this one time offer. Take this talisman from me, as protection from the evil of the forest and I will let you leave here. I will let you be the first to leave alive."

She then removed a necklace from around her neck and handed it to me. I tentatively took it, remembering what her finger nail had done to my face before, my stitches now burning and itching as she moved closer. Once it was in my hand I looked at the decorative designs on the ornate piece of jewellery. It was ancient. I saw that it opened, more of a locket than a talisman, and popped it open.

Inside I found two black and white photos. The one on the left side was of two adults, a man and a woman. The man was wearing a sharp looking suit with a top hat. He had a large black mustache. The woman was seated below him, his hand on her shoulder. She was wearing a dress that looked very much like the one the ghost girl had on before him.

The other photo made my heart ache. It was of the devil girl. She was wearing the same dress she had on now. In the photo her face wasn't decayed or rotten. In the photo she had on a smile that would light the darkest day.

"Is this you and your parents?" I asked, finding I sniffing back some tears.

"That was my birthday gift. For my tenth birthday. The day my life ended and this hell began."

I reached out and without thinking put my arm around her shoulders and pulled her in tight. I pushed the stink of death and the feeling of pus below my fingers away, as I comforted this lost soul.

She wiped her tears away from her face, taking away a large section of her nose.

"Thank you. Now please, go. Before the evil decides I have shared too much and decides you must die."

I snapped the locket shut and slipped it over my head, letting it settle around my neck. I looked at her one last time, but saw the little girl had left and in her place was the demon bent on revenge.

I took off running as fast as I could, hoping I was heading in the direction of the lake. Hoping to make it back to Vanessa and Sarah before the evil did.

18.

It had been too long. The boys should have made it back by now.
Vanessa and Sarah were still huddled around the dwindling campfire,
praying for their return.

"What do we do if they don't come back?" Sarah asked. Her leg
was getting worse. It already looked like it was turning gangrenous.
Vanessa was only in high school and had no idea if that was possible,
but she was fairly certain that it wasn't normal.

"I don't know. I think we wait here until sunrise. Then, if they still
haven't returned, we hike back to town and call the police. Sound
good?"

Sarah nodded and leaned over, letting Vanessa take her weight.
Vanessa had never been this scared. Not when Andrew died, not when
she was in the car when someone rear-ended them, not once had she
ever been this scared. And Jason. *Her* Jason. She wished and hoped he
was safe and ok.

From the trees before them the soft strains of music wafted towards them.

"Do I hear a piano?" Sarah quietly asked, her body tensing up.

As if on cue as an answer, a cloaked figure swept into view, sitting before a large piano made from bones. Behind him a sickening parade followed. Sarah and Vanessa sat horrified as they realized what they were watching.

In the front was a small girl, wearing a flowing dress. She was performing some sort of slow waltz by herself. Directly behind her was a group of people, their faces gone. In place instead were massive horns, protruding grotesquely forward. Vanessa noticed that a few of them appeared to be coated in fresh blood and gore. Next up was their friends Mason and Jen. Both were skipping and when the two girls realized what they were using as ropes both turned and vomited.

Behind Mason and Jen, David and Gavin appeared. David was screaming loudly, staring at his hands held out before him. Vanessa saw that he no longer had hands. Most of his forearms were missing, now just chunks and shreds of skin hanging awkwardly from the limbs. Gavin lumbered along as though fighting the effects of a tranquilizer. He swayed back and forth, almost to the tune of the song. His chest and abdomen were splayed wide open, the circular shapes letting the girls know just where the gore on those horns came from. Bringing up the rear was the missing hiker, Karl Radler, who appeared to have been burned severely.

As the loathsome group arrived before the two girls, the little girl up front gave a dramatic wave of her hand and the cloaked figure immediately stopped playing the piano.

"*Ta-da!*" The little girl squealed in delight as the music stopped. She turned back to the death marchers and clapped, giving her thanks for their performances in her grisly display.

"*Look at you two supple virgins seated before us. Thank you for being such a captive audience. You know, we are always looking to add new acts,*" she said before licking her lips slowly.

Vanessa realized that Jason wasn't amongst them. Her heart

sank. *But no*, she thought, *what if that means he's still alive?*

"*Are you wondering where your love is my dear?*"

Vanessa wasn't sure when the child had moved up so close to her,

but now that she was an arm's length away, her smell was

overpowering.

"Is he alive?"

"*He is. For how long? Who's to say?*" She laughed then and

twirled, before snapping her fingers.

The piano began to play again, the melody enough to make the

buried dance within their graves. Vanessa took a step backwards, away

from the group. She tried to get Sarah to move with her, but the girl

was firmly rooted.

"Sarah," she whispered, "Please, we need to move." She tugged

again but still no movement.

"*Shall we dance?*" The demon asked Sarah, pulling her away from

Vanessa. The two began to pirouette across the beach. Vanessa knew this would be her only chance. Seeing her dead friends in the lineup sealed it. She knew she couldn't save Sarah. It was either try to grab her and they both die, or leave now and maybe she would live.

As the little girl pulled Sarah around faster and faster, the figure's skeletal fingers moved in a blur across the bone appliance, the music picking up the pace. Vanessa ran.

She heard the party of dead howl behind her as she sprinted away from the camp site and through the trees. She didn't know where Jason was, but she hoped he had decided to try and leave. She didn't hold it against him. If he figured they were all dead, then just maybe he was trying to save himself.

She heard the group begin to give chase, the music never fading with distance. She didn't know how or why she wasn't making any progress from the group, but she believed it was because of the mystery of McConnell's Forest. A forest she didn't think she would ever make it out of alive.

19.

I hoped I was running in the direction to leave. I didn't think anyone else was alive. The talisman the girl had gifted me felt heavier on my chest, the chain around my neck now digging in. This feeling led me to believe I was travelling in the right direction. The further from her, the heavier it would grow.

As I burst forth from the trees onto a pathway, I was shocked to slam into a moving body. I flew to the ground and rolled over defensively, expecting something to start attacking. Instead I was elated to see it was Vanessa.

"Vanessa? Is that really you?"

As she struggled to make her way to her feet, I was expecting her to turn and show me that the girl had already gotten to her, had already stolen her to the other side. When her eyes met mine and I saw her full on, I knew that wasn't the case.

"Jason, oh thank god!" She grabbed me and hugged me tight, then peppered my face with kisses.

"We need to run, they're coming," she said then, and grabbing my hand, we fled.

Behind us the otherworldly strains of the piano caught up, and when I stole a glance back, I saw the horned boys bearing down on us.

We had so far to run. We weren't going to be able to keep up this pace. Then I felt the gift around my neck begin to grow warm. The stitches on my face began to grow hot and I felt them burning into my skin. I stopped and fell to the forest floor, letting forth an agonized scream of pain.

"Jason? Jason? What is it?"

Vanessa came back and knelt down beside me, trying to see what was wrong and how she could help.

Then a third presence joined us. Reeking of decades of rot, the girl's tongue slithered across Vanessa's face then cascaded over to my stitches. Her tongue flicked up and down, eagerly caressing the medical twine.

"Oh Talisman, Oh Talisman, thy guardian of time,

Oh Talisman, Oh Talisman, bring to me what's mine."

In one swipe of her clawed hand the girl severed Vanessa's head from her body. It dropped to the ground with a wet smack, her eyes rolling up and away from me. I looked at her face as her mouth moved, trying to speak words that would be forever stuck in her central nervous system.

"VANESSA!" I shrieked grabbing her head and feebly trying to put it back onto her body.

"Why? Why? Why? Why?" I rambled as I tried to line up the bloodied stump of neck back with the rest of her body.

The girl was laughing so hard at my frantic display that she was bent over, holding her stomach with one hand while her other hand was slapping her knee.

The parade of dead behind us was also laughing, although the dead sporting horn faces sounding closer to chess pieces clattering over on the board.

"I wore that Talisman when I was raped and murdered, you ingrate. You think you talking to me was enough for me to let you live? You skin-bags and your sense of morals."

She reached over to Vanessa's body and stabbed her hand into her chest, removing her heart. She did it so smoothly it was though it was a hot knife carving through butter.

Looking me square in the eyes, her tongue extended from her dripping mouth, and caressed the apex of the still pumping muscle tenderly. Then she swallowed it in one gulp.

That was when I gave up.

There was no hope left. Without Vanessa there was no purpose. Without Gavin, Mason, David, Sarah or Jen, how was I supposed to carry on? I had already lost Mikey. Now to lose all of my friends. My life had lost all meaning.

"Sip from the nectar of your love, my boy. Come, join me forever as my prince and let us dine for eternity on the souls that we steal."

"No."

My abrupt answer caused her to cower from me. Seeing the moment of weakness I stood, ready to stand my ground.

I should have known she was just playing with me. Whatever this *thing* was, that resided inside the body of this girl, it wasn't scared of anything.

It reared back and slashed me with both hands, sending me flying backwards. Searing pain scorched across my face and stomach. The weight of the amulet around my neck now so heavy it kept me from raising from the ground.

The demon child straddled my chest, hiked up her dress over her scabbed and decayed knees, then knelt down so that her face was only an inch from mine.

"*Jason, Oh Jason, you silly wretched boy. Listen to the sounds around you. Do you hear that? The bells are ringing. Can you pay the toll? Jason, Oh Jason, you silly morose soul. Listen to the trees around us. Do you fell that? The darkness is calling. Is it time to go?*"

She grasped my hand and pulled me to my feet. While she was singing to me, Vanessa transformed and had retrieved her head. She was now standing at the back of the line beside the dead hiker. She was holding her head in her hands, so that it rested between her breasts.

I tried to walk away, to take my place in line at the very back, but the small child was still holding my hand and wouldn't let me budge.

"*Silence greets the dead. Can you hear their speech? I thought not. For you still reside within the world of the living, sweet peach. Front of the line, until we get to the end of the path.*"

20.

We walked. I was in the front, beside the apparition of the urban legend of McConnell's Forest. The girl who hid in the trees.

Behind us was the pageant of the gored, led by the cloaked figure playing the piano. The music both soothed and sodomized my brain.

Marching in single file behind the music man was my dead brother Mikey, Vanessa's brother Andrew and the rest of their dead friends. They were followed by my best friends, the girls, the hiker and then my soulmate. The thought of her walking for eternity holding her head in her hands dropped me to my knees several times. Each time the demon-child yelled *'UP'* and I would return to my feet and carry on.

As the sun began to rise on my living nightmare, all of the members of the marching troop faded away, leaving me with the piano man and the girl.

As the threnody continued to emit from the instrument, the girl took my hand and led me to the edge of the trees.

When we reached the end of the path, the gravel parking lot a footstep away, she pulled me to a stop and motioned for me to stoop down.

I found she was smiling at me, once again masking what lie beneath.

"Jason. In over four hundred years, you were the first to speak to me like a real person. The first to acknowledge me as though I wasn't going to gut them. I can only repay you in one way. I will let you live. But sadly you accepted my Talisman, and I am sorry for my jest. You see the Talisman is cursed as I. So we are connected from now until death. You will see me from now, until your dying day. But I promise you, and please believe, no more pain will come your way."

She then pushed me hard out of the trees and I fell backwards onto the ground. Immediately I found the weight of her gift disappear from around my neck. The piano faded away and I was left alone.

I scrambled to my feet and began to walk briskly away, before turning and looking back.

There behind a tree was the girl, half hidden from view. When she saw me looking, she excitedly waved, which I hesitantly returned.

I watched as she faded from view, but I knew that wasn't the last I would ever see her.

21.

Over the decades since, I have grown to become an old man. I never left town, never got married, and bought a house near the gravel lot.

No one has been reported missing or found dead in McConnell's Forest since that fateful night. I would like to think I was a part of that.

Every day, I walk a loop that brings me back around by the parking area, then over to my house. As I approach I always know I will hear the piano playing, the music heard only by me. When I near the entrance to the path, I stop and wave at the girl hiding in the trees.

School kids still speak in hushed tones of the legends surrounding the area. Occasionally someone talks of seeing her ghost on a hike. A few pieces of clothing and scattered camping gear have been found over the years from our sojourn, but no bodies have ever been discovered.

To appease our friendship and keep the curse at bay, I spend a week every summer, camping deep with the woods.

By firelight I am joined by the dead. We dance, sing and reminisce of the old days. The days when they were alive. I snuggle in close to Vanessa, longing for her touch to be warm, but accepting the coldness no matter.

Maybe when I'm dead we will be together. Who knows? All I know is that for that week, I'm the happiest I've ever been. I suspect I'll join them sooner than later. Just need to work up the courage.

"Oh Jason, Oh Jason, come join us over here,

Oh Jason, Oh Jason, we wish you were near.

Oh Talisman, Oh Talisman, you may keep my curse,

Oh Talisman, Oh Talisman, lay him in thy hearse."

END

Afterword

Well thanks for stopping by to check out this quick tale!

This one was a unique experience for me. In 2018 I read a fantastic book; Tamer Animals by Justin M. Woodward (who I'm proud to call a friend now). After reading his urban legend, coming-of-age spectacular I wrote a short paragraph to myself that simply said; 'urban legend, coming-of-age, creepy, grotesque. Time to get super dark Stred.' Then I let it sit and marinate. Then one night I came up with the idea while giving my son a bath. Not sure why it came to me, like most ideas, it just did. Where I grew up (which I frequently reference in my releases) we had a ton of old buildings, old farmhouses that were just left to rot and decay. They always freaked me out. So this started to get my thoughts going. The abandoned farmhouse idea though has been done to death, and by far more capable writers than I. Additionally, one of my favourite songs ever and favourite music videos ever is 'Her Ghost in the Fog' by Cradle of Filth. So I wanted to write something that would fit into that imagery. If you caught it, I even mentioned her ghost in the fog in one scene! So I changed my details. The next day I wrote the entire story on my lunch break. I let it sit for a few days, came up with some edits, and then tinkered with it. Didn't take long and here it was!

This tale reads as though it could possibly have a follow up in the future, but as of this writing, I really have no plans to do that. Some stuff naturally demands a sequel, while others should be left alone. I'm finding that with my other novella Wagon Buddy. I have received a ton of requests to release a follow up piece for it, and I just don't think I can do it justice!

I want to thank David Sodergren for his ongoing hard work, making my stuff readable! Every message he has ever sent me has made me a better writer. Big thanks to Mason McDonald for yet another killer cover (most folks have said this is their fav one of my releases!) and thanks to J.Z. Foster for all your continued support and guidance!

Sincerest thanks to J.H. Moncrieff for your amazing advice and willingness to answer my odd questions!

Thanks to Gavin Kendall for the fantastic foreword. Can't thank you enough mate for all of your ongoing support and your tireless efforts to promote all things horror!

Extra special thanks to Deb Gillis. Her Instagram page is absolutely phenomenal and her photos of my books have been mind-blowing. Her constant enthusiasm towards my releases has been amazing and I am forever grateful for the support you've given me. Please make sure to follow her at dlgillis20 over on the gram!

To everyone who read it already to help with the pre-release promo, thank you so much!

2019 looks to be a fantastic year and I'm excited for the ongoing support! If you're not following me on only one or two of the platforms, thanks! If you want all my shenanigans;

Stevestredauthor.wordpress.com
Facebook.com/stevestredauthor
Instagram: stevestred
Twitter.com/stevestred

Cheers!
Steve

As promised, please enjoy these three short stories for some additional reading pleasure!

This quick story is maybe the first time I've written anything that could be considered cosmic horror. Maybe not? I'm honestly not too sure, as some of my releases walk a very fine line and could be perceived as cosmic horror. Either way, this one is a straight forward cosmic horror tale.

I came up with this during the Christmas break. One night I was lying in bed, not able to sleep. I currently co-sleep with my son, so I had my phone within reach and while he snoozed, cuddled up to me using my right arm as a pillow, I emailed myself draft #1. The idea came from the sky above. I couldn't tell you why it popped into my head. It just did haha! I had this picture of an old man staring at a corn field, while above him the clouds churned. So fifteen minutes later, draft #1 was done and emailed to myself. Few small tweaks and voila, here you go.

So please enjoy 'Abraham, Look to the Sky.'

Abraham, Look to the Sky

"How long you says he's been sitting there?"

Zack took a second, spit out a wad of chew through the open pick-up window and looked out at the fields beyond.

"Mah says'sm going on twenty years least. Say'sm he's convinced the sky gonna go dark, that heaven's gonna turn tah hell, and then we's done for," he replied, listening to the trucks engine clatter. The RPM gauge worked decently well, so when Zack saw the needle popping up and down between five hundred RPM's to three thousand and back, he knew it was past time to get some work done on it.

He knew he also wanted to feel Hazel's massive set of jugs again, so when she asked to drive out to see the old man sitting at the t-intersection in exchange for whatever he wanted, he readily agreed.

Now here they sat. To their right; cornfield. Fifty acres of Jeremiah's finest. Still months from harvesting, but it was all Zack could do to not jump out, rip a cob off and just eat it raw. Jeremiah often bragged about his farming prowess, and for once Zack wasn't going to call the man out for making up some bullshit.

Straight ahead; the dirt road. It stretched out for another twelve miles before it crossed over into the states jurisdiction and became paved.

To their left; the other section of dirt road. It travelled away, surrounded by wheat fields and cows.

And sitting there facing the corn field was old man Abraham.

He had hauled a wooden chair out to the intersection years before the red stop sign had even been installed.

Now he sat, day in and day out, long piece of wheat sticking out of his cracked lips. His cowboy hat was three sizes too big and his jean overalls hung loosely around his leather-bound frame.

Having never worn a shirt a day in his life, the sun had done a number on his skin.

But there he sat. Whether kids raced by him, spraying him with dust or rocks, whether the ladies from the church brought him lemonade and begged him to repent his sinful thoughts, he sat. Abraham wasn't moving for no one.

As he daydreamed about the crazy old man, Zack heard the passenger door close and he realized Hazel had exited the truck. She was now walking towards the senior.

"Ah, fuck a duck," he exclaimed as he climbed out, not even taking the time to turn the truck off.

As he jogged to catch up, he heard Hazel start to talk to the old man.

"Hey mister, whatcha doing?"

Abraham turned and studied her for a minute. Zack thought she'd make quite a study. Forty years old, straggly bleach blonde hair, eight kids from eight daddies, her stomach hanging out from the bottom of her tank top, looking like it might devour her short jean skirt. Hazel had already removed her dentures in the truck, prepping for some fun with Zack, so now her words were terse when spoken.

"Hey mister, don't mean ya no harm. Just curious about you sitting here in the sun's all."

At this Zack saw the man's body relax and he turned to look at the duo.

"Doing my wife's bidding, if you two must know. See's that there?" He pointed to the clear, cloudless blue sky above. They both nodded.

"Just before she died and cancer claimed another one of its victims she said, 'Abraham, look to the sky. For when the world ends the beasts will come from above.' So now's I wait. They're a comin', I'm sure of that."

Then ole Abraham turned back to the corn, leaving Hazel and Zack with their mouths hanging open.

When they got back in the truck, Zack finally spoke.

"Well, there it is. He's crazy. I didn't the stories were true but..."

Hazel began to rapidly shake Zack's arm, getting his attention.

"What the fuck woman?" He asked but then saw what she was pointing at.

Old man Abraham was now kneeling on the dirt road, arms extended above, as though waiting on an angelic hug.

"The sky..." Hazel whispered, still shaking his arm, "It's turning black."

Zack craned his neck over to see what she was yammering on about and sure enough, the once pristine sky was now completely covered in the darkest, thickest clouds Zack had ever seen.

"We need to leave," he said, but didn't move. They sat there as the sky opened up and the first rain in two months fell upon them. They didn't move when Abraham stripped naked and began to 'bathe' himself with gravel, making his thin skin slice open and bleed. And they didn't leave when the lightning began to pierce the clouds and then stab the land all around them.

Zack thought Mother Nature was putting on quite the show. Then Hazel began to scream. She screamed so loudly the rear-view mirror cracked and Zack was convinced his ear nearest her had burst. Hazel screamed to such an extent that her voice box shredded and blood poured forth from her mouth, drenching her shirt and cleavage.

Zack didn't care. For he was fixated on what Hazel was screaming at.

The clouds above Abraham, the nude, bleeding nut-job had parted. From that opening a dozen massive tentacles had descended, the enormous, round suckers flexing and opening, searching for contact.

When they finally arrived at Abraham, he embraced their communion, even as the thick hook within punctured his body.

As the man was hoisted skyward Zack simply sat, staring in disbelief, Abraham's screams growing quiet as he ascended.

The man's wife had been right. And as the skies opened and more

and more tentacles came to end the world, Zack looked to the sky as

well. Zack looked for his saviour to come and pluck him from obscurity.

END.

This tale is the second short story that appears after The Girl Who Hid in the Trees. I submitted this to a few spots and unfortunately neither place snagged it. Oh well!

This story fills two voids. The first was that it filled a twisted fairy tale void in my literature. I always wanted to write a bit of my own take on those childhood stories we grow up reading.

The second was that it fills a gap in my own writing timelines. I have a number of characters that appear and co-mingle within my short story world and even as far back as Jane: The 816 Chronicles. So this is a short story that ties together some stuff from Left Hand Path: 13 more tales of black magick and leads into my novel out at the end of the year The Stranger. You can read this story without having read any of my other stuff, which is great, but for those who have, you'll recognize the character I refer to right away!

The Tooth Collector

It was the sound of him giggling that made me pause.

"Jeff have a friend over?"

I casually asked my wife the question while unloading the dishwasher.

"Not that I know. I was going to ask you the same thing," she replied, rearranging the plates in the cupboard, trying not to let me see her fix my mistake.

"You know, it's ok if different sized plates touch each other," I chided, smiling at her OCD.

"You know, it's ok if you put them away properly the first time," she smirked back, goofy grin plastered across her face.

"Stop that, it hurts!"

I looked at my wife.

"Did Jeff just ask someone to stop hurting him?"

"I think so. Maybe go peek on him?"

I replied to her question by walking over to the basement door.

"Jeff, hey, maybe you guys stop rough housing so much?"

I half yelled it down, not committed to heading down the stairs. *Maybe I was lazy, maybe my knees ached, I could justify it to my wife*, I thought.

She wasn't buying it.

"Jason, just go down there. Don't be so lazy."

I huffed and started down the steps, when I heard the basement door open.

"Jeff stay inside, ok bud?"

When I got to the bottom of the steps and rounded the corner to the large play area, I found my son sitting on the over-sized couch, holding his right forearm.

In the middle of the room, one of our laundry baskets was laying. It was flipped upside down. The formerly folded laundry was discarded by the wall.

"Jeff, what the hell? Your mother is going to flip her biscuits when she sees that you unfolded all of these clean clothes."

Jeff looked up at me, all three feet of him. He was maybe forty pounds, turning 4 in a month. He was on the verge of crying.

"Jeff, hey, it's ok bud, why the tears?"

I went over and knelt down, and he started sobbing, pointing towards his forearm.

"Did you hurt your arm?"

Jeff nodded, hand not leaving its place. It was grasped firmly on his thin arm.

"Ok. Well let me see. You know I have special parent healing powers, right?"

Jeff nodded again, cheeks lined with water streaks.

Slowing raising his hand off of the area of concern, I let out a long whistle.

"Wow, bud that looks horrible. Whatever will we do?"

My son's arm had a small scratch on it. Whatever had scratched him had not broken the skin.

"But daddy, the serpent says its teeth have poison."

Huh, now someone has taught him the word serpent. Great.

"Some do, yes that is correct. But many don't. Many snakes can bite you but nothing will happen. Just an ouchie and then a mark. Were you outside playing and a snake decided to make you lunch?" While I should have been angry at Jeff for going outside unsupervised, I believed the snake had done me a favour and taught him a lesson.

"No, daddy. The serpent was playing hide and seek with me. It had the basket on its head."

Jeff than ran over, grabbed the basket and put his head in it.

Wearing it like a hat, he made growling noises.

"Oh, I see. Very scary."

Jeff kept doing it, waving his arms wide, hands shaped like claws.

"Well, how did the door open?"

I walked over, took a quick glance outside, before shutting the door and locking it.

"The serpent went outside when it heard you come downstairs."

"Well that makes sense," I replied, walking back to him.

"Have you healed up now? Or is the poison still flowing in your veins?"

Jeff lifted his arm up to show me. The mark was already gone.

"Ok, well there we go. Now let's head up and brush our teeth. It's getting close to bed time."

I let Jeff head up the stairs first. I wasn't sure why, but I waited until I was all the way upstairs to turn off the lights.

*

Over the next number of days, my wife and I heard Jeff playing downstairs. I had filled her in on what he had told me. She was adamant she never taught him the word serpent. So we both assumed maybe Sesame Street had worked its magic.

From time to time I would sneak down a few steps. Just enough

to take a quick look, make sure Jeff was not up to anything he shouldn't

be. My wife wondered why I was being such a helicopter parent. I

couldn't explain it to her. Something had just felt wrong with my

interaction with Jeff that night.

*

Three weeks later, we heard Jeff playing with his friend again.

"Jen, did you know Jeff had a friend over?"

I knew the answer before she replied, but for peace of mind, I

asked anyways.

"I was just going to ask you."

This time, I wasn't going to announce myself to them.

I went outside, onto our deck, and then using our family selfie-

stick, lowered my phone down, so that I could film the basement from

outside.

I pulled the stick back up, after a few minutes of recording. I went back inside and took the phone off of the stick.

Pressing play, I wasn't expecting the footage to have anything on it, other than Jeff.

At first the video was out of focus, showing the side of the house, our patio furniture by the back door, the bushes and the ground. Then it turned to face the window looking into the basement play area. I paused it.

"Jen, get over here. There *is* someone playing downstairs with our son," I whispered, not wanting to be so loud that they heard me downstairs.

"What do you mean?"

"Just get over here, now."

She hurried over and I pressed play again, angling the screen so that she could also see.

The video started again. In the basement play area, Jeff was running back and forth, keeping a good four feet of space between his little body and the hulking mass of whoever was down there with him.

The thing had our laundry basket over its head, obscuring what it looked like, from the shoulders up. From the shoulders down, it resembled a homeless person. It was wearing tattered, dirty rags, which were layered on its body. The shape of Jeff's playmate reminded me of a hulking wrestler or bodyguard. Large shoulders, thick back, muscular arms. With the white, plastic laundry basket over its head, it looked like it had been plucked straight from a comic book and placed in the basement.

I was scared to my core. The dread I felt, washed over me, making my vision go blurry.

"Jason, you need to go downstairs right now!" Jen was shaking.

I put the phone down, and looked at her.

"Call 911," I said as I went quickly to the garage. I grabbed one of my golf clubs, a 7 iron, and headed to the basement.

As I started down the stairs, I let out a guttural yell, holding the club as high over my head as the ceiling would allow.

As I got to the bottom of the steps, I heard the back door slam shut.

Entering the play area, Jeff was standing over in the back corner, looking in towards the wall.

There was no sign of the large person on the video. I rushed out the basement door, and spotted our laundry basket over at the edge of the yard. A larger area of the bushes was pushed away, appearing to show where someone had went through.

Jogging back in, Jeff was still standing in the corner, Jen crouched down beside him.

"Ok Jeff, who was that?"

I tried to ask it without sounding angry or scared, but my voice wavered.

"He says it was the serpent," my wife replied, half hugging him.

His tiny body was crammed so far into the corner I wasn't sure how he could even breathe.

"Why is he still in the corner?"

My wife gave me a look, a subtle way indicating that I should drop it, but I was fired up. *Who the hell was in our house?*

"Jason, just go upstairs. Give us a minute please."

I understood.

I went upstairs, returning my golf club to my golf bag.

I was sitting at the kitchen table when a knock at the door caused me to jump. Opening the door, it occurred to me that Jen had called 911. Standing before me was a tall, skinny man in an expensive looking suit. His face was off-putting, and I found I was having trouble looking directly into his almond shaped eyes.

"We received a phone call that there was an intruder in your house?"

While the man spoke, his head darted back and forth, looking past me, surveying the house.

"Yes we did, but I scared them off. Is it just you? Wouldn't more officers respond to an intruder call?"

I found it very odd that only one man was standing here. He had a white, four door sedan parked out front, half on the sidewalk. It didn't even appear to be a police car.

"Your wife was on the phone and said you scared them off, so the call was downgraded. I am here to investigate. Gather some clues."

Makes sense, I thought, *still doesn't feel right.*

"Where is your wife and son?"

"In the basement," I pointed at the stairs, "my wife was just calming our son down."

"Excellent. Wait up here please. I want a minute alone with them, and then I will get your statement."

The tall man proceeded down the stairs, and when I watched him walk, I felt a shiver go up my spine. He was decidedly creepy.

After thirty minutes, Jen, Jeff and the Detective all came up the stairs, Jeff looking ashamed. It was then that I noticed Jeff had some blood on his chin.

"Dad, your son would like to apologize to you."

I knelt down, making sure I was at Jeff's eye level.

"Ok, whenever you are ready Jeff."

Jeff slowly looked up, bottom lip quivering, eyes covered in a shallow pool of tears.

I felt my heartstrings get plucked and I engulfed him in a hug. I didn't know what was going on yet, but I knew he was scared.

"Daddy... it was the serpent. He made me open the basement door. Then when you came down, he made me stand in the corner so I wouldn't be able to watch it disappear."

"Oh Jeff, I am so sorry. Did the serpent hurt you?"

I leaned back a bit, wanting to see his face. I didn't think he would lie to me, but if he was that scared you never know.

"No, it didn't hurt. He just told me that one tooth will do."

My eyes went wide, looking over at my wife. She was looking out the front window and I could see her eyes were cloudy as well.

"Jeff, can you open your mouth?"

Jeff slowly opened his mouth, which let me see that his left central incisor had been extracted.

Before I could say anything, the man in the suit gently pulled on my shoulder, getting my attention.

"Jason, please, let's let your wife and son have a moment, get cleaned up. I need to get your statement."

I stood up and followed the man outside to the deck. My wife went over to the sink, running a cloth under the water. We locked eyes for a minute and I knew what she was telling me.

I don't trust this Detective.

I gave her a slight nod, and returned my attention to the man, as he started asking me questions.

The tall man asked me a number of questions, and I went through the narrative of what had happened, up until the knock on the door.

The entire time, I kept noticing something was reflecting in the back yard, shining in my eye. It was sitting near the section of the bushes at the back, where something had forced its way through.

"Anything else Jason?"

"Huh? What? Sorry, I zoned out for a second," I replied, forgetting for a few moments that the man was still here.

"Nothing. It's ok. Here is my card. If you think of anything else give me a call."

I took the card and the man left, making some small talk with my wife. I heard the door close, and then looked down at the card.

It was completely blank except for a phone number. The number had an area code I wasn't familiar with.

My wife came out to the deck.

"We need to talk to Jeff. That thing took one of his teeth. He said that it was going to return tomorrow for more."

I pushed by my wife, headed down the stairs, through the play area, and out into the backyard.

I rushed to the section of bush, searching for the item that had been reflecting.

I dropped to my hands and knees, searching with my hands for an object.

"Jason, what are you doing?"

I heard my wife behind me, heard her approaching, but I didn't stop or reply.

Jackpot.

My right hand connected with something hard and sharp. Picking it up, I stood up and held it out to inspect.

As Jen arrived she let out a startled squeal.

I was holding a tooth. It was three inches long and came to a sharp point with a slight curve. One end had traces of blood on it, indicating it had been recently removed.

There was no doubt in my mind that this was a snake's tooth.

*

Sleep wouldn't come.

I tossed and turned, the vision of that tall man and the snake's tooth playing over and over in my mind.

I listened to my wife and son sleeping peacefully. There was no chance Jeff was sleeping in his room alone tonight, so we had made sure he came and slept with us.

Every creak, every groan of the house made me listen intently. *If I was ever going to have super powers, now would be ideal,* I pleaded.

My eyes grew heavy, my limbs became light, and I drifted off.

The large shadow moved in the hallway, coming to a stop at our door.

*

I woke up the next morning to screams.

Bounding out of bed, I found my wife on our bed, chin covered in blood.

She was screaming while Jeff sat shaking beside her on the bed. He had pulled his legs up in tight to his body, arms wrapped around them.

"Jen are you ok?" I asked, as I rushed around the bed to her side.

She tried to speak. At first only blood and spittle came out, a tangy orange-tinged fluid leaking out of the sides of her lips. Her face looked like she had been electrocuted; lips trembling, eyes wide, her nostrils flaring.

"My teef are... my teef are gon," she finally stammered. She opened her mouth to show me. All of her teeth were gone, her mouth was now just rows of bloody gums.

She began crying, screaming, shaking and while I tried to calm her down, I was glancing over at Jeff. His eyes were blank.

"Jeff are you ok?" I asked as I tried to get Jen to stand up. We needed to take her to emergency right away. Or a dentist. I honestly didn't know.

"The serpent was here. It made me stay quiet. I'm sorry I peed the bed."

I glanced down and saw that Jeff had peed the bed.

"That's ok, you were scared. Come, we need to take your mom to get help."

Jeff begrudgingly made his way off of our bed and followed us down the stairs. I grabbed the car keys and we went into the garage.

We quickly backed out and drove away.

In my rush, I didn't see the white four door sedan parked across the street.

The tall, skinny man in an expensive looking suit was smiling a wide smile, mouth filled with bloody teeth.

*

There wasn't much they could do for my wife. They did emergency dental surgery to clean up her gums and work to prevent any infection. Once she was healed we would begin the process of dentures.

When we got home late that day, Jen fled to our bedroom, slamming the door behind her.

I looked down at Jeff, who had waited patiently with me all day at the hospital.

"You want some food buddy?"

Jeff just nodded. He looked so exhausted, but I was still proud of how well he had handled the long wait at the hospital.

I warmed up some leftovers we had in the fridge and once the microwave dinged, I used some gloves to take it out.

"Here we go," I said, before realizing I was alone in the kitchen.

I could see the glow of light coming from the basement.

I didn't even hear him go down there.

"Jeff?"

I took a few steps towards the basement, when I heard my son's voice.

"Please don't hurt my daddy, you already hurt my mommy," he pleaded.

I froze. I expected a reply, but when Jeff spoke again, I realized that whatever was down there with him was communicating only to Jeff; it wasn't allowing me to hear it speak.

"I promise, I promise they won't do anything else. Just take my teeth and don't hurt them, please?"

I could hear my son crying now. This got me moving.

I ran down the stairs as fast as I could, taking the steps two at a time.

As I landed at the bottom something solid hit me in the face, sending me sprawling to the floor.

"Daddy!" Jeff cried out.

I shook my head, trying to get my bearings. Looking into the play area, I saw the hulking creature carrying my son over its shoulder.

It was walking towards the open door and Jeff was struggling, but it was no use.

His tiny arms and legs kicked and punched, but the creature was far too big, far too strong for Jeff to have any affect against it.

"Jeff," I yelled, getting to my feet and running after them.

I left the house, spotting the two of them half way across the back yard. Jeff was still screaming and pleading for me.

As they got to the bushes at the edge of the yard, the creature finally turned and looked at me.

Behind them, the bushes parted and the creature held up my son. In one smooth movement, like a magician pulling a tablecloth off, it used one clawed finger and removed all of my son's teeth. The creature then turned and tossed Jeff through the opening.

"JEFF!" I screamed, rushing towards the creature. As I got close, I went into a crouch, ready to tackle it. When I made contact, I immediately regretted the decision. It felt like I had impacted a cement statue.

I bounced off, feeling my left shoulder dislocate, arm hanging limply.

As I lay on the ground, trying to work through the searing pain coursing through my body, I watched in disgusted astonishment as the creature threaded my son's teeth through a thin piece of string or wire. The creature pulled the thread from somewhere in its rags, then took the time to wet the end. It then used its strength to force it through the cracked molars. It then wrapped the wire around its neck, making a macabre necklace out of the teeth.

From behind me a scream erupted, and looking up at the deck I saw my wife Jen.

The scene below her was too much and she collapsed to her knees.

"I'm sorry Jason," a voice I instantly recognized, spoke from behind me, "but we needed the boy. Don't worry though. We didn't forget about you."

The tall, skinny man in the expensive looking suit walked around from behind to face me. He motioned with his hand, and the massive creature with the reptilian face moved forward.

It picked me up easily with one hand and I was mesmerized by its tongue darting in and out of its mouth. With the hand holding me, it began to squeeze harder, forcing me to take a deep breath, opening my mouth wide. In one quick movement with its other hand, it ripped all of my teeth out, the loud pops of each molar leaving my mandible sounding like gunshots through my skull. Once done it dropped me.

"Good work serpent. Now come, the boy is still crying."

The two then walked through the bushes, my wife still screaming on the back deck.

I made my way to my feet, saliva and blood now pouring out of my mouth. My arm still dangling, lifeless.

I grunted and groaned as I forced my body through the bushes, just in time to watch the four door sedan slowly pull away from the sidewalk. Jeff was in the back, face and hands pressed hard up against the window, screaming for me.

The tall man was driving, and seeing me, gave a friendly wave, bloody toothed grin covering his face. There was no sign of the creature.

As the car drove away, Jeff's screaming diminished, eventually fading to the point where I could no longer hear it.

My mouth was now on fire, my body responding to the extraction of all of my teeth.

I could hear my wife screaming still.

I felt something hard in my pocket. Reaching in, my hand closed around the snake's tooth I had found.

The end was sharper than I was expecting and I felt it prick my finger, causing a warmth to rapidly spread up my arm.

I knew I was in trouble immediately. Jen's screaming grew fuzzy and distant and my vision began to spin.

As I dropped to my knees, feeling my lungs growing warm and my heart beating furiously in my chest, I remembered something Jeff had said that first night.

"But daddy, the serpent says its teeth have poison."

As blood began to pour from my eye sockets and ears, I knew that the serpent hadn't lied to Jeff.

I just wish I had known the meaning then.

END

So here we are! The last tale of darkness included in this release.

So The Navajo Nightmare was originally submitted to Flame Tree Press for possible anthology inclusion, but unfortunately wasn't picked up. So I've included it as the third story joining The Girl Who Hid in the Trees and it's the fourth one here.

This tale also filled a spot for me. A supernatural western story. I've previously released two western tinged stories; Time Out Noose and Too the Moon – Sadness. Neither had any supernatural elements. So here we are, me scratching that itch.

This one also really hit home for my love of horror themed westerns. So this story will be the intro story leading into (hopefully) the 2020 release of a full length novel, co-written with another fantastic writer, using the same title; The Navajo Nightmare. I'll keep you all updated as progress goes along!

So enjoy this fun ride!

The Navajo Nightmare

The belt hung preposterously low, as though it was being pulled straight to hell by the hands of his dead.

He couldn't fully close his hands, the nails having been recently removed. Dried blood flaked off as he flexed his fingers, his mouth curled in a grimace as the pain scorched through his nerves.

He knew shortly he would need to strike, but for now he was a shadow, hiding in plain sight.

The revolver stayed coiled in the holster, like a rattlesnake waiting to strike.

"You going to stand and stare all day, or we going to get to some killing?"

The voice yelling from the side of the crowded street had the effect he was looking for; his challenger glanced, for less than half a second, towards the yeller. It was all he needed.

The air was cut through with a crack, as the pistol blasted, and the challenger dropped dead in the street, the middle of his forehead turned into a bay window.

"Arrest that… that thing!"

The sheriff bellowed loudly as a group worked to pull the dead lawman from the dirty road, but it was too late. The Navajo Nightmare was gone, disappearing before anyone could grab him.

*

The tale of the Navajo Nightmare began with low-whispers in the back of bars. Bandits spoke in hushed tones, telling the story of an outlaw, an Indian with his face painted white with red lines through his eyes, who would suddenly appear. The horse he rode was 17 hands high, and could run faster than the trains across an open plain.

As the legend grew so did the mythology; he had been captured by Soldiers and was forced to convert, only to seek vengeance. Others said that his family had been captured and scalped, so now he sought each person involved one by one. One person surmised that he painted another red line on his face after each kill. The only thing that anyone could confirm to be true was that the Navajo Nightmare was the fastest draw hands down. There was no one even close.

Which is why Robert was contacted. You see, Robert was the fastest gun in the west. Or so the billing on his marquee said. He would travel around, following the circus circuit and make a few bucks in each town. He would do the ole shoot an apple off someone's head, while they were both blindfolded, and he would shoot five random items thrown into the air before any of them touched the ground.

You see, the Navajo Nightmare's latest victim was none-other-than Deputy Billy Johnson. And just who was Deputy Johnson you ask? Well he was the son of the Vice President. So Robert was contacted and then contracted to hunt down the Navajo Nightmare and kill him once and for all.

So on a breezy October morning, Robert and four other lawmen met up to help track their suspect, set off, heading towards the unforgiving foothills several miles out of town.

*

That first day, the five men had high hopes. None of them believed the stories that had been passed around about a ghost Indian, a native walker back from the dead. How could they? For if you were dead, would you not shoot imaginary bullets? No, they believed this man to be just that, a man. A man with face-paint, a big horse and an accurate shot. Robert didn't even think his shot was very fast. He made the assumption that because people had built the shooter up so much that they simply froze and were surprised with the display before them.

Nope, Robert told the other men, he would shoot the Navajo Nightmare before the man even knew they were there.

The four lawmen appreciated the realism of the showman, but in truth, they were all a little nervous. They were not so sure that Robert himself wouldn't freeze, when faced with the very real threat of death. They had decided not to tell Robert that in order to find the Navajo Nightmare, they would be heading deep into hostile territory, and worried he might tuck tail and run.

That first night, the men made camp near the base of the foothills. The lawmen had all brought rucksacks to fashion makeshift hammocks. They knew the area was teeming with rattlesnakes and didn't want to risk being attacked while sleeping.

This was something Robert was unaware of, so he spent the night restless and uncomfortable trying to sleep on his horse.

*

The second morning of their 'adventure' as Robert had called it, was met with the first sign of trouble. For when the group woke up, they discovered that there was now only three lawmen remaining. The fourth had simply disappeared in the night, leaving his horse and belongings.

"This doesn't make sense, why would he just walk off?"

"Maybe he woke up to take a piss and simply got turned around?" Robert's presumption was something he had heard could happen, but the other men had none of it.

"He has 25 years of guiding service to his record. He would not simply get turned around. He was taken. Something was here, the air tastes foul."

The group packed up quickly, taking the missing man's horse and belongings with them. They couldn't find any trace of the man, or any tracks suggesting someone else had been there.

"I don't like this one bit," said the largest of the lawmen. Robert detested that they wouldn't tell him their names, but tried to not let it bother him.

The men rode in silence for the next several hours before stopping for a drink and a late breakfast. Finally Robert couldn't stand the anonymity anymore.

"So tell me," Robert asked, "why won't you tell me your names?"

The three remaining lawmen all smirked at the question, before the largest one, and the one Robert now assumed to be the leader replied.

"So tell us, showman, what makes you believe you can ask that question?"

This caused the three of them to burst out laughing, slapping their knees and snorting.

"I don't find this funny at all. The Vice President has personally asked me to track down and kill the man responsible for his son's death. And you three laugh at me?"

"Calm down showman. We are just trying to lighten the mood. For the day will grow darker before the night comes, we can assure you of that. Now to answer your question. I was born with a name, but when I went into service training they strip you of it. We are all trained to do one job and that is protect the law and our country. We are all lawmen and as such do not need an identifying name. If you must, you may call me John. That there is William, and the fellow beside you is Butch."

"Thank you. I appreciate that."

"Now let's move out," said John, "the terrain grows rough and the territory will grow dangerous. Keep your eyes sharp and your wits about you."

The four saddled up and headed off, unaware of the watching eyes from above.

*

The rain came unexpectedly, but with no worry of a flash flood. The group decided to leave the missing lawman's horse behind, as the ground turned muddy. They didn't want to risk it slipping or falling. A broken leg out here was a death sentence for a horse.

Robert found himself lost in the beauty of their surroundings. For the last decade he had been limited to his train car and the stage in each city. His schedule was such that he had very limited down time and any chance of being a tourist disappeared as soon as the show was over. Now though, he found himself mouth agape, staring at the hills jutting up all around them. He was so entranced that he almost didn't see that the three ahead of him had come to an abrupt halt.

"Why did we stop?" he asked.

"Quiet. Voice down." John snapped back and then motioned for the lawman behind him to move. The lawman, known to Robert now as Butch, jumped off his horse and made a slow approach ahead of

John. Robert couldn't see what was in front of them, but he could see William was frantically looking around the hills.

Robert leaned over to get a better view and was repulsed with what he saw.

The missing lawman was propped up in the middle of the path ahead. He was still in uniform, but he was missing his face. The grinning skull stared back at the crew, arms pulled out beside him, like a poorly made human cross.

"He did this," Butch said, as he arrived at the dead man. "What should we do with his body?"

"Leave it. The buzzards will pick it bare and we don't have time to stop and bury him. Let us say a prayer for his soul and move on."

Butch and William both said Amen and Butch returned to his horse. Mounting it quickly they moved on. Robert couldn't take his eyes off of the skull face as they rode by, the flesh completely removed, the white of the bone like porcelain.

*

That night they decided to sleep in shifts, with someone staying awake, keeping guard. It was agreed that Robert would simply sleep, as they wanted him rested and alert, should his quick draw be needed the following day. To nobody's surprise, Robert didn't fight against the motion and went to sleep immediately.

"Great, we are in the presence of a coward," William spoke, as the three men filled their lips with chew and passed around a flask. "Hush," John replied fiercely, "any man who saw what was done to our lawman back there and didn't turn and flee has some courage in him. I just hope he doesn't lose it when we need it most."

*

Robert woke the next day, glad to find all men were accounted for.

"Saddle up. We will eat at lunch. Until then we ride. I suspect our mercenary is stationed near the waterfalls at the old gulch. I have heard reports that some wagons have been robbed near there and the suspect had a painted face."

The three lawmen and the showman rode silently, focused on ending this, bringing some justice to the murdered son. They knew the Vice President would be forever grateful.

*

As the sun arrived at the height of its path, the gang of men neared the gulch. Robert had never seen a waterfall before and was excited to see one in person.

A whistling noise pierced the air and William was thrown clear of his horse. The force of the arrow threw him ten feet off of his stead and the projectile went clean through his body.

"Attack! Down, down!" John yelled and Robert and Butch pitched off of their horses. In their haste Robert realized he only had his pistol, his rifle still holstered on the horse.

From above the men rocks began to rain down causing them to scramble, trying to find a safe place to hide. An alcove in the hill offered them refuge from the barrage.

"That can't be one man," Robert said, sounding like he was on the verge of crying.

"I don't believe so, no. But whoever it is doesn't want us to get to our man. We have been followed for some time now."

As quickly as the rocks had started they stopped. The men slowly made their way back to their horses, who luckily had stayed.

"Alright, that's the second sign trying to prevent us from continuing on. I suspect the third attempt will be the most vicious of them all. Butch, kick William's body into the river. Maybe in death he will rot and ruin their drinking source."

John swatted his horse's rear end with the leather strap and started out ahead, while Butch went over to William.

"Until we meet again," he said, pushing the body into the water. Getting back onto his horse, he gave a quick salute then motioned for Robert to get moving.

Soon they would come face to face with a living nightmare, but once again, none of the men looked above to see the watching eyes.

*

On the last day of their journey, the men found themselves at a literal crossroads.

"Which way should we go?" Robert pondered, looking at the path to the left and then the path to the right. Neither path looked like it had been recently travelled.

"We will head to the left. I have heard reports of an old miners shack up this way. To me that makes the most sense for a hide-out. There isn't a lot of traffic coming through this way, most travelers stay to the flats and it's only a half days ride out, to get more water or if you were going to rob a caravan."

John spoke with such authority that Robert saw no reason whatsoever to question the man.

The three got their horses moving and followed the left hand path. As they went the path began to gradually grow steeper, working its way up the side of the hill.

"The miners shack is close. Guns out fella's, we need to end this quick."

Robert pulled his rifle from the holster. His pistol was always close to his hand and would be pulled from its resting place with the speed of a thousand men. He was confident in his abilities. Over-confident some would say.

As the group approached, the shack was spotted. John motioned for them to stop, and they all dismounted. John waved for them to follow and the two kept close to the man as they ducked down and hustled over behind a row of rocks.

"Someone is in there. See the smoke coming from the chimney and a pair of boots at the door? Butch, you flank the shack around the right side. Robert, you stay put here, while I take the left hand side. When I am in position, I will yell, and when that door opens, Robert, you end this."

Butch and Robert nodded, understanding the orders.

John went to the left, Robert stayed crouched behind nature's fence, while Butch took off to the right. Robert found he was breathing heavy now, adrenaline firing through his body. He laid the rifle down on the ground, knowing this wasn't the gun he was going to use.

"YOU IN THERE! THIS IS THE LAW! COME OUT NOW!"

Robert hadn't realized it was going to happen so soon. He stood, turned, and the moment a figure emerged in the darkened opening of the shack's door, he put two bullets between the man's eyes. The figure dropped dead on the front stoop.

"Yahoo!" Butch yelled out, running from his hiding spot. A loud bang echoed through the close confines of the hills and Robert watched as Butch's head exploded behind him. He looked around, trying to get eyes on where the shot came from but it didn't make sense. The shooter would have been right in front of Butch?

"John, are you ok?"

Robert yelled out to the remaining lawman, but got no response.

Ducking low to the ground he shuffled over towards where John would have been, but found nothing when he got to the spot he assumed the man to be at.

"Where are you John?"

A crack echoed loudly and searing pain ripped through Robert's right leg, dropping him to the dirt. Looking down he realized he had been shot, the muscle blown open and the bone fragmented below.

Screaming he pain, he frantically waved his hand around trying to find the shooter, when he realized that he had dropped his pistol when he fell.

He quickly found it near his side and as he reached for it a large, bare, scabbed foot slammed his outstretched hand to the ground. Looking up he saw John leering down at him.

"John... what...?" He stammered, trying to piece together the man before him.

"Robert. The word is a cruel, bitter place. I actually was growing to like you. Even as a showman. Any last words?"

"You? You are the Navajo Nightmare?"

The man chuckled, seemingly pleased with the nickname. He then proceeded to reach up and peel away the face of the lawman named John, exposing a white painted face with red paint down his eyes. Casting off the clothes, the man was left exposed, causing Robert to gasp.

The Navajo Nightmare was missing large chunks of skin, exposing rotting organs and yellowed, decaying bone beneath. A leather skirt worn loosely covered the man's groin but that was all he was wearing. Long thick black hair adorned his head, but Robert could see a small line of blood near the scalp.

"Is your hair not even real?"

The living hell before the showman grabbed his hair and peeled it back. The scalp struggled to let go, thick strands of pus and flesh hanging on for dear life. It finely let go with a slurping sound, exposing a yellowed skull and leaving behind chunks of skin.

"Robert. I have been dead for hundreds of years. Ever since my family was slaughtered. A relative of yours was there. He held the axe. He took my scalp and took my life. Now, I take yours."

"I challenge you to a duel. Let the faster man live."

"Showman, I would normally accept your challenge. But not today."

Then the Navajo Nightmare pounced, his Tsenil maul high, crushing Robert's skull.

Robert died with his hand on his gun, too slow to stay alive.

Reaching down, the man stuck two fingers into Robert's pool of blood, then brought his hand to his face. Pulling his bloody finger down, the murderer streaked another red line through the white paint.

The Navajo Nightmare then turned and walked by the shack, past the dead miner with two bullet wounds between his eyes and the dead lawman known as Butch. He then stopped, put two fingers in the sides of his mouth and whistled loudly.

A massive beast of a horse appeared from the hills, 17 hands high, missing large chunks of its flesh. The man hoisted himself onto the stallion and kicked the animal's sides hard. The horse galloped forward, before the two figures disappeared into the shadows, on the hunt for more retribution.

END

One final note here from me.

As an indie author, it can be tough to get my work seen by people who enjoy reading this type of book.

Once done, whether you loved it or hated it, please, please go leave a review.

Amazon, Goodreads or Book Bub is ideal. Facebook, Instagram, Twitter works just as well.

Lastly, I want you all to read my stuff and love it. If you bought this – thank you so much. If you snagged it on promo, that works as well. If you want to read more of my stuff but simply can't afford it, by all means, head to your local library and request it.

Cheers!

Made in the USA
Monee, IL
23 June 2021